# WEST BOTTOMS

**By Rogers Brazier and Mace Thornton**

Ebook ISBN: 979-8-9911560-9-7
Paperback ISBN: 979-8-9911560-7-3
Hardcover ISBN: 979-8-9911560-8-0

Library of Congress Control No. 2024923045

Original front cover illustration of police revolver by Hayley Brazier. Back cover historic photo of West Bottoms courtesy from Missouri Valley Special Collections, Kansas City Public Library, purchased and used with permission.

Personal Chapters
PUBLISHING

*Independence, Mo & Wakarusa, KS*

# DEDICATION & ACKNOWLEDGEMENTS

To my brother-in-law, Rogers Brazier Jr., I owe a huge thanks for believing in my quirky idea of a tag-teamed novel. Writing West Bottoms was an enjoyable and engaging work of creativity. Your input and enthusiasm were invaluable in bringing our characters to life, and I couldn't have asked for a better collaborator.

To my wonderful wife, Denise—your unwavering love and support have meant everything to me throughout this process. Thank you for sharing those delightfully broad and colorful anecdotes about a few very distant relatives; they sparked my imagination and brought unexpected layers to the story.

I also want to express my deep appreciation to the many people I've met from the small towns of rural Kansas. As gritty as West Bottoms is on the surface, the best qualities of rural Kansans has shown me the true meaning of kindness and community, inspiring me to reflect that in my work.

And lastly, a small note of regret: I wasn't born early enough to experience the rough-and-tumble Kansas City of the 1930s, a time of renaissance, resilience, and larger-than-life characters. Through a whisper of their stories and history, we have tried to capture a glimpse of that remarkable era. This book is our tribute to that dynamic past. –*Mace Thornton*

*May 2022.* Baldwin City KS. Over lunch of Sonic burgers and fries Mace and Denise pitched Mace's idea the two of us work together on what would become West Bottoms. Thank you, Denise, for the unexpected call earlier that sunny spring day, and thank you Mace for the unexpected proposal and the thoroughly enjoyable collaboration of melding together a diverse collection of characters and events. Thank you, Mom and Dad, for allowing your teenage son to paint crazy stuff all over his bedroom walls, and for not painting over any of it until many years after he'd grown and left home.– *Rogers Brazier*

# WEST BOTTOMS

# TABLE OF CONTENTS

WEST BOTTOMS

## NANA'S STORY, PART ONE

**M**arch 2003. The young girl had blond hair - not short, but not long - and just enough curls to give it a naturally tousled look. Not bleach blond, but blond with a hint of orange. Mostly blond. Adult-style, pastel-framed sunglasses sat propped atop her head. Her eyes hazel green, set just the right distance apart. A woven cloth bag limply hugged one hip, hung by a simple strap slung across the opposite shoulder. One hand tightly grasped a leather portfolio against her slight frame. She walked hesitantly through open doors into the spacious lobby of La Casa Familia, Palm Springs' exclusive senior care home. Large ceiling fans rotated slowly overhead, barely stirring up a breeze on the almost perfect mid-March day. A baby grand sat silently in one corner of the room. Framed original oils of southwest scenes hung at proper spacing on facing walls.

The young girl soaked up the environment, then strode through the lobby past a smattering of disparate aged elders and middle-aged children huddled in hushed conversation, straight toward a well-dressed woman bearing a plastic name tag pinned to the lapel of her tan jacket.

The woman smiled. "Good morning, dear. May I help you?"

"Yes, thank you. Foxy Storm?"

"Of course." The woman stepped back, turned and nodded down a hallway. "You should find Ms. Storm in the day room. Halfway down."

The young girl smiled and started slowly down the breezy hallway, her steps echoing ahead. Without a disapproving adult in sight, she ran the fingertips of her free hand lightly along the rust-colored stucco wall before pausing at open French doors of a room furnished with round tables, cushioned furniture, a television, and potted palms, populated by several uniformed staff and maybe a dozen or so wheelchair-bound elders staring vacantly ahead, dozing off, all playing a role in the inevitable end-of-life saga. She rummaged through her bag, retrieving the recent photo of her great-grandmother, her mother's grandmother. The aging woman in the photo, eyes sparkling, teeth gleaming white, stared over a shoulder straight into the camera, absolutely owning it.

The young girl's eyes swept the sun-splattered room. There, alone in the corner, seated in a wheelchair with a view of the home's circle drive and portico, sat her great-grandmother. The young girl lurched forward, quickly weaving across the large room's Spanish tile floor. She reached the old woman's side, leaned forward, gently touching her shoulder.

"Nana."

Startled, the old woman turned quickly, paused, then broke into a broad smile, eyes sparkling just like in the photo. "Oh, come here, Sweetie," she said, arms outstretched. "Ahh, you're a great hugger. Sit down, sit down." Foxy Storm leaned back in her chair and studied the young girl for a moment. "My, my, my, you're all grown up. Not the little cutie I remembered. Do you still go by Meg?"

"I'm only fourteen, Nana. Almost fifteen. And, no, only Father still calls me that. I prefer Megan."

"Megan it is then," Foxy said matter-of-factly. "So where are your parents?"

"They dropped me off, then headed to the hotel to check in and play a set or two of tennis." Megan laid her portfolio and bag on the coffee table separating the two, then settled into an oversized arm chair. "They'll be here for supper."

"Perfect! It's you I've really wanted to see." Foxy reached into her silk blouse and pulled out a small lavender envelope. She removed a lavender card from the envelope and held it close to her eyes. "So, tell me about this writing assignment."

"Well, Nana, I'm in a creative writing class at the academy. Five thousand words, the subject of our choice." Megan smiled. "I want everyone to know about you, Nana. I chose you, your story."

"I see that," Foxy said, smiling as she returned the envelope and card to her blouse. "And you wanna be a writer someday, yes?"

Megan nodded.

"Well, I've been giving this assignment of yours a lot of thought, a lot of thought." Foxy paused. "So, this is really how you wanna spend your spring break, sitting here with an old woman?"

Megan wondered for a moment if she was being tested. "Nana, you sure don't sound old and, yes, there's no place else I'd rather be." She laughed. "I stomped my feet until Father agreed to fly me out here."

Megan realized she wasn't sure what she was expecting only a few minutes earlier, but she wouldn't have guessed at her Nana's vibrancy, her clarity, her eyes, subtly accented by a wisp of eyeliner. Her skin relatively taut with nary a wrinkle, a faint blush on her cheeks. Her voice, reasonably strong, though occasionally changing octaves like a boy coming of age.

Foxy smiled. "And you say most of it's already written?"

Megan nodded. "It's a draft, yes, but I need to fill it out with details only you know. Tidbits, insider stories, and your life after the movies."

"Very well," Foxy said. "I wanna hear everything you think you know, but first let's move out to the patio. Plop your things on my lap. You're driving."

Foxy scanned the room, locking eyes with Gonzalo, a broad-shouldered young aide who quickly joined the two. "Gonzalo, we're moving outside to my table. My Camels and my special lemonade, please."

In no time Megan had maneuvered her Nana outside to a shady corner of the patio, the view of others mostly obscured by a collection of potted, large-leaf palms. Gonzalo was right behind with Foxy's order. She looked at Megan. "Lemonade, Munchkin?"

Megan shook her head.

"Thank you, Gonzalo. Please stay close."

"Always, Ms. Storm."

Settled on the patio, Megan loaded and started her cassette recorder, and leaned back with notepad and pen. She shared snaps of overheard conversations while growing up that now made sense. She recalled understanding the Nana she barely knew had been something big, someone known, but the focus of little girls is usually elsewhere, Megan explained, not on ancient black-and-white relatives existing in frequently dusted photo frames scattered about the family's spacious Connecticut home.

But then it all changed. Five years earlier, on a Sunday morning over breakfast, Megan's parents informed her a handful of close friends would join them that evening for an intimate Academy Awards watch party. Megan could help tidy up the home and could stay up past her bedtime.

That evening Megan was privy to a flood of Nana stories, mostly from her mother, as the adults snacked and drank. It was all new to the little girl, and a bit much to absorb. Just in time the anecdotes and second-hand stories died away and a hush settled over the comfortable parlor room, interrupted only by crackling embers in the stone fireplace.

All eyes focused on the Sony flat-screen as the tuxedoed host dramatically described Nana's meteoric rise to fame, her career's evolution, her professionalism, the universal love on set from the grips to the director, how she famously demanded a list of all cast members before shooting began and made it her mission to know every member on a first-name basis before shooting wrapped.

And then, after twenty years as a beloved household name, Foxy Storm disappeared from the public eye. Save for a brief cameo without lines in a cookie-cutter 1960s beach movie, Foxy had moved on.

Tears born of unrestrained pride had already welled in young Megan's eyes as she watched a gaggle of well-dressed older men and women accompany her doddering, cane-wielding Nana across the Hollywood stage to be honored with the Academy's Lifetime Achievement Award. As the cameras captured the audience, every member rising to honor one of their own, a golden age matriarch of their craft, the dam broke, tears streaming down little Megan's cheeks. Her trembling lips gave way to uncontrollable sobbing and a comforting embrace by her teary-eyed, otherwise stoic mother.

"I had no idea, Nana."

Megan launched into a rapid-fire recitation of a young girl's driven quest to learn everything she could about her famous great-grandmother, from peppering her mostly patient mother with probing questions, hours spent with the incredibly helpful local librarian, to careful study of the seldom opened family photo albums.

"I've a snapshot memory of rolling on your lawn, with your curly-haired puppies licking my face."

"Oh my, Pumpkin, that must've been nine, ten years ago."

"Yeah, it was," Megan nodded. "We've got a picture of you, me, Mother and Father, but Mother doesn't recall who took the picture."

"Oh my," Foxy laughed, "you are the inquisitive sort."

"I know. Sorry. I'm always wondering 'who snapped the photo?' Drives Father crazy."

"I can imagine," Foxy smiled. "Hmm, I believe it was the lawn man."

"Oh, okay. Well, I recall another time we were together, Nana," Megan said. "I was seven, maybe eight. Mother had me all dressed up. She spent a long time picking out my clothes, fussing with my hair."

Foxy leaned back, smiling.

Megan continued. "It was a fancy restaurant in the city. White tablecloths, flowers on the tables, several glasses, lots of silverware."

"Oh my, of course, several years ago." Foxy paused. "Yes, we hadn't been together since your visit to Bel Air. I flew in the night before to see an old friend on Broadway, and then to attend a fundraiser the next evening, raising money from nice people with more than they can ever spend, trying our darndest to save the elephants."

Foxy tapped out a Camel from the soft-pack and fired it up, taking a deep draw. She lifted her mostly empty glass, swirling the melting ice cubes. In a flash Gonzalo appeared, taking the glass and disappearing just as quickly.

"Those cigarettes aren't good for you, Nana."

"Neither's the vodka."

"Nana!" Megan laughed.

"You're right, but they've had seventy years to get me. Ain't happened yet."

Megan smiled.

Foxy continued. "Nope. Go figure. What's gonna get me is this." She touched her waist. "My pancreas. Cancer. The doc tells me I'll go quick."

Megan absorbed the news slowly. "Oh, Nana." Tears pooled in the young girl's eyes. She fought the urge to blink, but did.

Foxy forced a smile and fished around for a clean tissue. One for herself, too. "It's part of the deal, Button."

For a moment there was silence as the two daubed their tears. Foxy spoke first. "Serendipity."

Megan looked up, puzzled. "I can spell it, but the meaning – "

"You're the answer to a question I didn't know to ask. That's what it means. And," Foxy laughed, "I just love that word, but I've so few opportunities to use it. It's what came to mind after reading your card."

Foxy continued, speaking seriously about facing her fleeting time and the torment of having lived a lie, her growing desperation to set the record straight, but uncertain of the best vehicle to do so.

"In our case, serendipity means you've answered my prayers." Foxy tapped her blouse. "With your card here all the puzzle pieces came together."

Megan looked uncertain.

"Cupcake, you dream of being a writer, an author. I'm blessed and flattered you're wanting to write about me." Foxy took a dramatic breath. "And boy do I have a story to tell."

"More than I already know, Nana? I'm pretty sure I've read just about everything written about you. Mother rolls her eyes when I ask – "

Foxy raised a hand. "It's mostly all a lie, Sweetheart. You're gonna need to start from scratch." Foxy winked. "Trust me, it'll be worth it, and I'll die knowing you're gonna set the record straight, give my momma the recognition she never got, write the true story of Nancy Gleason from little Pickford Falls."

"Who?"

"And Jimmy Dale Cooper."

"Wait, what?" Confused, Megan looked up from her notepad. "Big Jimmy? Grandpa Jimmy?" Megan hesitated. "The mafia guy?" she asked sheepishly.

"No, Muffin, my first Jimmy. And Big Jimmy always told people, told everyone, he was a 'businessman.'"

Foxy took a big drag and leaned her head back, blowing a blue-gray stream of smoke upward, her eyes far away. She told Megan of a frazzled Nancy Gleason arriving at Central Station on the east side of downtown Los Angeles, July 1934, with two battered suitcases – one stuffed with cash – and nothing beyond a fuzzy idea of what to do next. She hadn't bathed in more than two days.

Wandering through the bustling station the dazed redhead found a helpful railroad agent. The older man walked the young woman from Kansas out to the street and pointed. "Two blocks. Ask for the Widow Jenkins. She's from Kansas, too."

Foxy found the no-nonsense Widow Jenkins and checked herself into the affordable Downtown Women's Hotel, paying a week's advance for a small room and communal bath.

Flustered, Megan interrupted. "So, you're telling me you're this 'Nancy Gleason?' That's your real name? It's not Foxy Storm? The Pickens book said you grew up the only daughter of a widowed, wealthy Kansas cattle baron with, like, thousands of acres and a whole bunch of ranch hands. You grew up rich. Jack Warner spotted you in the train station after your daddy sent you here to pursue your dream. And, what's this about a suitcase full of –"

"All a lie, Dearie. Well, not the suitcase full of cash. But the other stuff was Hollywood glitter. Made up. That was a studio book for my fans, the studio's fans. Arthur Pickens was a hack." Foxy squished the Camel and tapped out another, savoring the first deep draw. "That wasn't fair. Pickens was a good enough writer, but he wrote what he was told to write, what sounded good to someone wearing a suit. And what sounded good to me, too."

Megan dropped her notepad on the table. "I've never heard of Nancy Gleason, Nana. Mother never said a word. Mother talked about the cattle ranch and –"

"She doesn't know, Cupcake," Foxy said matter-of-factly. "I lied to her. I lied to her daddy, rest in peace. I lived the fantasy. Guess I much preferred Foxy Storm's life. After a while it became my reality," she said, shrugging her shoulders. "Big Jimmy knew. I eventually told him, but anyone else who might know the truth is dead, long gone."

Megan stared at her notepad. "Nana, we need to back up. Tell me about the suitcase full of cash."

Foxy leaned forward. "Sweetie, what led to Foxy Storm was a stolen car. In Kansas City. Kansas side. A Ford. A Saturday night. July 1934. Just two stupid kids stealing a random car. Turned out it wasn't just any car. Without that stolen car, that Ford, there's no Foxy Storm, no movies, and I'm Nancy Gleason, Nancy Whatever, barefoot and pregnant, singin' in the church choir, and the Megan I'm talkin' to doesn't go to a pricey Connecticut private school."

Megan digested what she was hearing, her Nana's serious tone. She smiled. "Serendipity?"

Foxy laughed. "Hmm, well, maybe so, but it didn't seem so at the time."

## WESTIN HAWKINS, PART ONE

The rise to local fame and great wealth by Westin David Hawkins was another of America's unlikely rags-to-riches stories that, upon reflection, seem not so unlikely at all. From a young age Westin Hawkins expected to be "someone," though what exactly that meant to him early on was nothing more than a vague notion.

Born in 1880 to a deferential mother and the hard-working, second-born son of an Iowa farmer, Westin was just a little guy when his father loaded their possessions onto a wagon and moved him, his baby brother and pregnant mother to the northwest reaches of Dakota territory, land that was breathtaking and desolate at the same time. Westin's father staked a claim to 160 acres east of Medora, an aspiring town spawned from the plains along the newly laid tracks of the Northern Pacific Railroad.

Westin's mother gave birth to a third boy, followed in quick succession by a fourth and, finally, her precious baby girl. Over time a four-room wood home replaced the hastily constructed one-room sod dugout. A small barn followed. The original ten acres turned for corn doubled. A second draft horse, sheep and chickens joined the small herd of cattle. The family tended to the milk cow early every morning and early every evening, every day of the year. Each member of the family old enough to walk and dependably follow directions played an essential role.

In later years, Westin was unable to recall a time he wasn't scrapping with his younger brothers, neighbor boys or schoolmates before facing the expected wrath of his pious father, who finally reached his breaking point when his fifteen-year-old delinquent son sucker-punched then laid out his rural school's teacher, resulting in a permanent expulsion. Westin's exasperated father had long given up hope the couple's first-born would model the responsible behavior expected of a God-fearing young man. Westin was, to his father, regrettably beyond redemption.

## WEST BOTTOMS

The family's oldest son knew he'd done wrong, and didn't bother with a futile defense for the unprovoked beating of the persnickety teacher. He knew, too, given the chance, he'd do it again. That evening, as his younger siblings completed chores, Westin's father told the boy to leave. For good. Westin's mother handed him a knotted bundle containing a change of clothing, hard-tack and jerky, tied to a cottonwood switch, and covertly slipped into her son's hand four silver coins.

With a figurative shove toward manhood, Westin readily left behind his family and the only home he could remember, embracing his freedom.

With the silver coins jingling in the only pants pocket that didn't have a two-finger hole, Westin launched out on the two-hour walk to Medora. Arriving at dusk, the freshly liberated boy trudged aimlessly down the middle of tiny Medora's dusty main street. Midway through the two-block long mix of unpainted, clapboard business structures and weed-filled empty lots, Westin made an abrupt left-turn toward the sound of voices inside the single-story Golden Nugget.

Westin stepped through the open door into a narrow, deep room dominated along one side by a simple, polished cedar bar, and on the other by four round tables and chairs crammed together. The friendly bantering tailed off and heads turned as the boy, chest out, shoulders back, strutted straight to the bar, dropping his stick and bundle to the rough-hewn pine board floor. The half-dozen patrons returned to their small-talk and cards as Westin slapped a silver coin on the bar. "Whiskey."

The balding saloon's owner critically studied the unfamiliar customer with a man's height, but the face of a boy. "Hat off, young man," the owner said as he set a shot glass down in front of Westin and filled it full from an almost empty bottle of caramel-colored whiskey. Westin, hat in hand, jerked his head back as he downed the shot, the nasty liquor barely skimming the back of his tongue.

Westin's virgin throat reacted violently to the instantaneous burn that plummeted through his chest, doubling him over in a coughing spit, prompting raucous laughter from the saloon's regulars, all once novices themselves. The saloon owner poured a second shot, then a third, then a fourth, and with each succeeding shot of whiskey the burning sensation waned, and the warm buzz of intoxication grew.

Before Westin's fifth shot a dusty cowboy with tanned, leathery skin and a drooping salt-and-pepper mustache sauntered in and took a spot by himself at the bar's end near the door. The cowboy wasn't much older than Westin's father, but a lifetime on the range had aged him. He nodded generally to the others before dropping his worn Stetson on the bar, waiting quietly as a glass mug of foamy warm beer was brought to him.

Westin, feeling pretty cocksure by this time and itching for a fight, inched down the bar closer to the unpretentious cowboy, making one disrespectful comment after another. The cowboy ignored him, alternatively gazing into the beer he nursed or staring straight ahead. The background conversations in the saloon stopped altogether, and all eyes turned to Westin and the cowboy when the saloon owner loudly ordered Westin out of his bar. "It's alright, Johnny," the cowboy said, the first words he'd spoken since walking in off the road, "I need to be movin' along." With that, the cowboy picked up his hat and started for the door.

"Hey, mister," Westin said in his best menacing voice, "no one turns his back on me."

The cowboy paused, but without turning around or acknowledging the challenge, continued outside. Westin followed, catching up to the cowboy out on the road. The saloon's patrons and owner rushed to follow the two, gathering together on the rickety, wood-plank sidewalk.

"I think you're a scared," Westin sneered.

The cowboy halted, dropped his hat to the road and turned, facing the hotshot kid tight behind him. Without warning, Westin launched a haymaker at the cowboy's temple but whiffed badly, losing his balance when the cowboy fluidly leaned backward. Quickly catching himself, Westin turned and fired a left jab at the cowboy's jaw, but missed again when the cowboy sidestepped the kid's telegraphed punch.

Rebounding from his second misfire Westin wound up another haymaker, but never threw it. Fast as a lightning strike the cowboy's gnarly clenched fist fired out, hitting Westin like a sledgehammer in the middle of his forehead, knocking him off his feet and flat onto his back. The saloon's patrons, almost all of whom had spent time on the range with the cowboy and none of whom would've ever dreamed of picking a fight with him, howled with laughter and slapped backs as they ambled back inside the saloon, clearly entertained by the unexpected diversion.

The cowboy knelt down next to the unconscious kid and gently slapped the boy's cheeks, then poked a shoulder once, twice, a third time. Westin stirred, then opened his eyes to see a blurry, spinning cowboy lurking over him, staring back. Westin caught a strong whiff of the cowboy's chewing tobacco sour breath.

Still kneeling, the cowboy straightened up. "What's your name, kid?"

"Westin. Westin Hawkins."

The cowboy grabbed Westin's hand, turning it palm up. He ran his fingertips across the palm's wavy callouses. "Can you ride a horse?"

"Course I can."

"Herd cattle?"

"Yes," Westin lied.

"Well, I see you're not afraid to work," the cowboy said as he stood, offering a hand down and helping the wobbly kid to his feet. "I can use a ranch hand, if you're interested."

"Sure," Westin blurted out.

"Ever heard of the Maltese Cross Ranch?"

"Oh yeah," Westin lied again.

"It's a couple hours south," the cowboy said, walking toward his tethered horse. "We're leaving now. Grab your bundle. You can walk."

Over the next two and a half years the two worked side-by-side, the cowboy silently prideful of Westin's growth from a boy to a young man, no longer the troubled kid he first met. For his part, Westin came to embrace the foundation principles of his surrogate father to make a sincere effort every day, from the moment he awakened, to the time he fell off to sleep, to do right, be respectful, and to do nothing at all for which an apology might be required.

The cowboy was just a young boy in Canada when America's civil war erupted, but news of the death and carnage south of the border was constant and inescapable. Later, when he moved south into Dakota Territory, it was for opportunity and maybe a little adventure so long as he stayed far removed from senseless bloodshed, wanting no part of it.

Safely removed by more than a thousand miles from America's elites and power brokers in the east, the cowboy grew increasingly uneasy as word swept across the American West in February 1898 of the USS Maine explosion and sinking in Cuba's Havana Harbor. Rapt westerners consumed the inflammatory reports of movers and shakers in the east pushing for war, anxious that America flex its muscles and not pass up this expansionist opportunity. And Spain, formerly a dominant colonist but now on a downward slide, was just the right foe, regardless of whether it actually had anything to do with the Maine's sinking.

Unlike the cowboy who'd seen a thing or two, the headstrong son he never had was hyped up by news of the prospect of war with Spain. Despite his emotional maturation since the cowboy took him in, Westin was still just a seventeen-year-old boy, the age at which armies over the millennia had mustered soldiers to fight and die.

The cowboy did his best to tamp down Westin's heightened zeal when word reached the northern prairie the call had gone out for volunteers, but finally relented. Resigned to losing the boy, on a cold April night the cowboy sat down at the ranch house writing desk and, by the glow of an oil lamp, composed an unvarnished letter of reference addressed to the Maltese Cross ranch owner. Early the next morning over breakfast of eggs, bread and porridge, he handed the letter to Westin sealed in an envelope and addressed simply to "Mr. T. Roosevelt."

"They're raising a volunteer cavalry. This man," the cowboy said, pointing to Roosevelt's name, "will be one of its leaders."

Westin picked up the sealed envelope. "The ranch owner? The eastern tin foot?"

"Yup, the same. He's more than an easterner with money. He's an important man back east. I'll sleep better if you ride with him."

The best the cowboy could offer on how Westin might track down the future president was to show the young boy a dog-eared studio photo of the man dressed like a cowboy parody, "Washington, D.C.," and the "Navy Department."

Packing little more than when he left home almost three years earlier, Westin now carried changes of clothing in a worn canvas duffel bag instead of at the end of a cottonwood switch. He was soon traveling east with passage to Minneapolis. From there he hoboed his way to the nation's capital, eventually finding the gleaming tile hallway outside Mr. Roosevelt's office. Ready to pack it in after hours of patient waiting, Westin leapt to his feet when the great man finally emerged from his office with a bookish underling not much older than Westin.

A suddenly awestruck Westin rushed forward, holding out the cowboy's letter. "Mr. Roosevelt, sir," he said nervously, "this letter is from Butch at the Maltese Cross. North Dakota. I'd like to enlist in your cavalry."

Roosevelt stopped short, initially unsure of the disheveled young man's motives, then softened, eyeing Westin before accepting the envelope and silently reading the cowboy's straight-forward praise of the boy standing in front of him.

A grin spread across Roosevelt's face. "Bully good," he boomed, the words echoing down the deserted corridor. "So you're the hand about whom I've heard?"

"Yessir," Westin answered, assuming so.

"Can you make your way to San Antonio, haste speed, Menger Hotel?"

"Yessir."

"We're looking for cowboys from Indian Territory and the southwest," Roosevelt said, peering over his spectacles, "but we'll make an exception for Westin Hawkins." He turned to his young assistant. "James," Roosevelt barked, "back to the office for a letter of introduction our Mr. Hawkins can carry to San Antonio."

Little more than two months later Westin and most of the Rough Riders set sail for Cuba. A day after landing, the green troops were thrust into action at Las Guasimas, and one week later at the Battle of San Juan Heights, made famous by the valiant charge up Kettle Hill by the Rough Riders and several African-American regiments. Though not shot, bayoneted, or decapitated by cannon fire during his time in Cuba, Westin was, for the rest of his life, haunted by the eerie, insect-like sound of bullets whizzing all about him – "zzzip," "zzzip," "zzzip" – and the slug's soft thump when its flight was interrupted by a shoulder, a leg, a head, killing some, wounding others.

Despite the wretched jungle conditions and a lingering bout with yellow fever, Westin survived the "splendid little war," diplomat John Hay's snappy description of the brief action that led to armistice on August 12, 1898. Spain ultimately recognized Cuba's independence, ceding temporary control of it to America, and handing over Puerto Rico, Guam and the Philippines, formalizing America's emergence as a legitimate global power.

Two days following the armistice the now famous Rough Riders landed at Long Island, New York, and Westin, along with a number of others, was hospitalized for treatment of his persistent yellow fever. As his condition gradually improved, Westin devoted more and more thought to his future. Exposed to all types of characters since leaving North Dakota, having experienced the America about which he'd only read, an ocean and a war, he concluded that returning to the cowboy, the Maltese Cross, and a land where cattle and sheep far outnumbered people was not his destiny. Not that he had the faintest idea what that might be.

Westin asked for writing paper and ink, and composed a heartfelt letter to the cowboy, describing his adventures and explaining, best he could, why he wouldn't be returning to North Dakota. After effusive praise to the cowboy for turning him into a man with good character, a grateful Westin closed with a sincere promise to visit at his earliest opportunity. Though the two exchanged intermittent cards and letters over the succeeding years, never again did they see each other.

Before the Rough Riders disbanded in mid-September 1898, its troops scattered by the four winds, Westin picked one brain after another concerning his immediate future, speaking with anyone willing to give him the time. After the third or fourth strong suggestion, he set his sights on Kansas City. His mind was set: Westin Hawkins would give it a go in Kansas City.

Hoboing his way from the northeast, across the upper Midwest, then angling down toward the country's midlands, Westin worked every odd job he could find, but never stayed in one place more than a day or two, always moving toward his destination. He arrived at Kansas City's rapidly developing economic hub on an empty boxcar at midday in October 1898, unaware that less than a hundred years earlier Lewis and Clark had disembarked close by to visit a Kanza Indian village early in their exploration of Jefferson's Louisiana Purchase.

Westin knew little of Lewis and Clark, nothing about the Kanza or the arrival of French fur traders seventy years earlier, marking the beginning of the area's white settlement in what became known as the West Bottoms, somewhat of a cone-shaped floodplain. Fanning out along its north boundary was the Missouri River. High bluffs framed its east and west. The smaller, more volatile Kansas River flowed north below the west bluffs before emptying its muddy water into the Missouri. The valley included the state line dividing Kansas and Missouri, running north to the Missouri River.

By the time Westin hopped down from his boxcar the West Bottoms was well-ensconced as an economic heavyweight of middle America. A mere thirty years earlier, though, it was a sparsely-populated agricultural area separating–like a father separates a pair of brawling brothers–the nascent Kansas and Missouri cities sitting atop high bluffs, each desperately seeking its identity in a post-Civil War America. That all changed when Kansas City, Missouri grappled with upstream rivals Leavenworth, Kansas and St. Joseph, Missouri over the Hannibal and St. Joseph Railroad's proposed Missouri River rail bridge and won.

The first permanent rail crossing of the Missouri River was completed in 1869 and provided a direct line into and from the West Bottoms. The Hannibal Bridge soon carried the traffic of eight railroads, connecting the West Bottoms with the major trade centers to the east, making it a big-time player in the country's stream of commerce, initially with whatever might come off the plains farms and ranches but later diversifying with industry that started picking up steam shortly after Westin's arrival.

The West Bottoms boom started small in 1871 with a 13-acre stockyard along the Kansas River and the Kansas Pacific and Missouri Pacific rail lines, luring livestock from the west. The stockyards rapidly spread out, crossing the state line and, along with meat-packing and the growing rail traffic infrastructure, dominated the West Bottoms' southern end. To the north of the stockyards, growth consolidated initially around the enormous, palatial Union Depot, which opened in 1878 to great fanfare and was soon surrounded for several square blocks by an eclectic mix of saloons, gambling halls, brothels, lodging, schools, and churches.

Industry followed, staking its claim to the north end of the West Bottoms, producing all manner of packaged food and product that might be loaded on rail cars and shipped out. Myriad businesses ancillary to industrial expansion followed, adding to the thousands of workers who descended upon the West Bottoms each day, most of whom might bathe once a week on a Saturday evening and who, in any event, didn't bathe before going to work.

Westin, duffel bag in hand, soaked in the beehive of humanity moving to and fro, drawn forward by the edifice dominating the landscape, the colossal Union Depot. Dodging pedestrians, horse and carriage, and slow-moving steam engines, Westin rubber-necked his way past the European-looking train station and toward an unmistakable odor–the odor of livestock. Trudging south several city blocks Westin was soon surrounded by all manner of corralled livestock–cattle, sheep, hogs, horses, mules. Essentially, almost anything on four legs raised in rural America. Within an hour Westin had landed a job in the stockyards as a drover, expected to report early the next morning.

With but a few silver dollars to his name, and not certain when he'd have enough to board a room longer term, Westin figured he'd search out a nearby saloon, have a meal, and return to bed down for the night in a remote cranny among the labyrinth of corrals. A couple hours later, the autumn sun long gone, Westin sat alone nursing a frothy, warm beer at a table in the dining room of a hotel close by the stockyards, the hotel being one that catered to drovers, railroaders and other working men.

It was pushing toward late when a well-groomed, olive-skinned young man strolled in and went straight to the bar. He stood out like a sore thumb. Decked out in a coat, tie, bowler hat, flashy garnet ring and a brass-tipped walking cane, the young man, not much older than Westin, waited patiently as the portly, mustachioed bartender retrieved, then handed to him a thick white envelope. The young man slid the envelope into a coat pocket and, with a smile and tip of his hat, turned and headed back out onto the dimly lit sidewalk.

Much of what Westin had seen his first day in the West Bottoms was eye-opening, odd, different, and the thirty-second appearance of this dandy ranked with the rest. Returning to his beer, Westin noticed across the room three unsavory-looking characters grab their hats and swiftly abandon their table, moving quickly toward the door, leaving unfinished their latest round of drinks. Westin was certain a robbery, maybe a beating, too, was about to go down. His diminished, but not yet extinguished, attraction to a good fight, coupled with his acquired expectation of fair play, pretty much drove him to his feet in hot pursuit of the likely scoundrels to insure they left the olive-skinned dandy unharmed.

Westin looked left, then right, as he reached the sidewalk. He just caught a glimpse of the three shadowy figures as they scurried around a corner of the hotel and into a dark alley. Westin rushed to the alley, sliding to a stop at the alley entrance. Ahead, maybe twenty paces, the dandy stood facing the three menacing characters, their backs to Westin. The dandy raised the walking cane to shoulder height as the three men spread out, moving slowly forward.

"Stop!" Westin shouted, getting the dandy's attention as the three men spun around.

Westin dropped his jacket to the ground as he walked forward, immediately singling out the group's probable leader as his target, the man in the middle. Westin lunged forward and landed a straight right to the man's nose, a left uppercut following like a blur, snapping back the man's head. Before Westin could land a third punch he was blindsided and tackled by another of the men, both flying to the ground.

As Westin landed his first punch the dandy jumped forward and with a swift flick of the wrist whacked the third man across the top of his head with the walking cane, staggering the would-be robber before he crumpled to the ground in a lifeless heap. A second whack with the cane across the temple of the man flailing backward from Westin's punches dropped him to the ground.

24

Westin and his attacker quickly separated, each scrambling to his feet. With no hesitation the third bandit fled down the alley, disappearing around the hotel corner.

Ten seconds after it started, the brawl was over. Westin, his clothes a mess and short of breath, turned to the surprisingly calm dandy, not a hair out of place, who fished a business card from his vest pocket and handed it to Westin.

Westin twisted his body to catch enough light, reading the card aloud. "Thomas Lozarro, Businessman."

"You know, Mister, uh - "

"Hawkins. Westin Hawkins."

"Mr. Hawkins. Thank you. You know, Mr. Hawkins," the dandy continued, "maybe I handle two of 'em, but three might've been too much." He smiled. "Good thing we'll never know."

The dandy reached out his surprisingly calloused hand, the vice-like grip Westin would've expected from a North Dakota cattleman shaking on a deal for a prize bull. "Call me Tommy. I've a business not far from here. I'm headed there now. Join me. We'll talk."

"My bag's inside," Westin said. "I'll go grab it."

# WEST BOTTOMS

# SUMMER 1933, A SCHEME IS BORN

It was lunch time. Monday, July 9, 1934. Kansas. Yet another dry, brutally hot day. Beasley Wentsworth sat at a small table in the back room of Macy's in downtown Topeka staring at the bland meat sandwich he'd made at home before leaving for work, his mind racing. Fifteen minutes earlier all was peachy-keen. But then he'd been told by his women's wear department supervisor there was an emergency call from a cousin. The caller, actually his only friend, not his cousin, had delivered the bad news and a slow, serious warning, and Beasley was understandably freaked out. He easily envisioned the worst-case scenarios. His inconsequential life ruined. His stern father and loving mother absolutely crushed. A respectable future gone forever. Prison. Chain gangs. The cops always got their man. He was in a boatload of trouble.

He'd been reminded not to panic, not to run, not to admit anything, and for God's sakes to burn everything as soon as possible. Every frickin' scrap of paper. Burn it all. Make sure his share of the cash was hidden really, really well. Remember, he was told, this was certain to occur at some point. It's just happening a little ahead of schedule. Stick to the plan and he'd be okay. Yeah, right. Beasley pushed the sandwich away.

A year earlier, a mere two months into a relatively cushy job with the Kansas State Treasurer's office, Beasley's telephone rang.

"Good morning, this is Beasley Wentsworth," he'd said with the arrogant tone of a young political appointee who'd burrowed into a job not based on experience, competence, but rather due to the quiet influence of someone with actual clout.

"It's true!" the familiar caller's voice exclaimed. "You son of a bitch. Look at you now."

"For goodness' sake, is this Gabe? Gabe Hawkins?"

"The same, buddy. How ya been, Beez?"

"I'm good," Beasley answered. "How long's it been? Two, three years?"

"Who gives a fuck," Hawkins laughed. "I'm in town. Let's grab some lunch. Meet me at the Jayhawk Hotel in an hour. I'll get us a table."

Looking back on that fateful day, Beasley realized he wouldn't have both feet in a pile of crap now if he wasn't still awe-struck of the older Gabe Hawkins. Six years earlier Beasley had been a scrawny, pre-pubescent freshman at Kansas City's exclusive Pembroke Hill School, scared to death of the older kids and incredibly desperate to find a safe niche for himself.

He tried football in the fall, mostly serving as a tackling dummy during practice. He went out for basketball in the winter, and even on a freshman boys team of seven players he rarely left the bench. He hated running, so he passed on track in the spring and reported for lacrosse on the first day of practice. His life would never be the same.

Gabe Hawkins, senior captain of the defending city league champion lacrosse team, took notice of the shy kid who didn't speak or make eye contact sitting alone in the corner of the locker room as Coach Driscoll droned on about unselfishness and pride. After the team hit the field to work out, Hawkins approached Beasley and started peppering the rapt freshman with questions. "Who's your dad? What's your dad do? Where do you live? Any sisters? Brothers?"

The next day in the crowded lunchroom Hawkins got up from the cool kids' table and walked to the far corner where Beasley sat by himself picking at his green beans. "Hey, freshman, come join us."

After that, Hawkins became the older brother Beasley never had. And, Beasley wanted to believe even now that Hawkins, an only child, had found the little brother he'd always wanted.

Even after Hawkins left for college the two stayed in touch, mostly with goofy letters and post-cards, but also with soda shop meetups and ballgames when Hawkins was back in town for the holidays or summer break.

Like many friendships, though, real world life drove a gradually deepening wedge between the two. Hawkins spent his college junior year in Europe, and soon after his return became enthralled with a Boston debutante. After several months without contact between the two, Beasley received a brief letter from Hawkins with a clipping from the Boston Herald social news page mentioning the two lovebirds. Hawkins didn't return home from school that summer, and Beasley caught a train for college on the west coast not long after graduation. After an extreme bout of homesickness, and against the pleas of his parents, Beasley soon boarded a train for home, choosing work over higher education.

Over the next several years the two friends would occasionally talk or exchange letters, but serious face time was limited to a one-time chance meeting at a Monarchs ballgame one hot summer evening, followed that night by the two stumbling drunk onto a downtown sidewalk after closing down one of Kansas City's hopping jazz clubs.

Beasley ran a comb through his thick dark hair, straightened his tie and checked his watch before pulling open one of the Jayhawk's heavy brass and glass doors and ascending the stairs to the lobby. Off the dark wood-paneled lobby was the elite restaurant, filled by noon every business day with the state's politicians and power brokers. Anyone who was anything in Kansas dined at the Jayhawk. Scanning the cloth-covered tables, Beasley saw Hawkins' waving hand from a table in the corner. With shoulders back and head straight, Beasley weaved through the crowd of middle-age and older white men, doing his best to pretend he belonged amongst them.

Hawkins smiled, rising to greet his friend. "Hey, buddy, it's great to finally see you again. It's been too long."

The two young men took their chairs as a waitress arrived with glasses of water and a drink menu. "Scotch and water for me," Hawkins told the waitress. He looked at Beasley, who smiled and shook his head. "A soda for my friend, please."

Beasley watched the waitress turn and leave. "So, Gabe, what the heck brings you to Topeka?"

"Actually, I'm here to see your dad, and a few other senators. They're workin' on a bill that'll help the economy. There's a word here 'n there we need tightened up, but it's almost ready to drop." Hawkins took a sip of water. "Your dad's been a great help. He hasn't told you about it?"

"Nah, he's pretty tight-lipped about stuff. We don't talk much about what he does here in Topeka." Beasley laughed. "Hell, we don't talk much about anything. He and Mom are just glad I've got a regular job and can pay the bills." He laughed again. "They've had plans for my room for a long time."

"You've got great folks, Beez. Say," Hawkins added, "I've got lunch today. Keep that wallet in your pocket."

Beasley started to protest but didn't put up a real fight. He was a mid-level public servant, at best, living in a tiny apartment near the State Capitol building. No car. He walked to work. Otherwise, he took a trolley or bummed a ride. He was saving for a decent used car, but it was going to be awhile. Beasley was squeaking by, able to set aside a few bucks each month, but paying for lunch at the Jayhawk, or even his share of it, would've set him back at least a month or two. "Thanks, Gabe. It's on me next time."

The two men talked through lunch, and were still talking after their plates were cleared and the restaurant emptied out.

"So, you spend all day in a corner of the vault, recording bond serial numbers, checking for signatures, blah, blah, blah?" Gabe asked. "No offense, Beez, but it sounds kinda boring. Way below ya, buddy."

"I know, I know, but I've got my foot in the door. This is entry level stuff, Gabe. Gotta pay your dues, right?" Beasley said, then added. "Plus, there's a bunch of folks right now, and not just the grease monkeys, who can't find work."

"That's true, Beez."

Looking back months later, Beasley honed in on this part of the conversation as the point where the genesis of his life's downward spiral took seed. He just didn't know it yet. Who could've known it? At the time, telling the best friend he'd ever had about a new development bond program seemed totally harmless and, he thought at the time, maybe more than a little interesting to someone on the outside. Heck, it was totally harmless. And double heck, it was interesting. It was state government doing what it could to help the thousands of desperate, out-of-work Kansans who were losing hope, not waiting for that goddamned communist FDR to ride to the rescue. Beasley was darn proud of what the State was doing and here was an opportunity to share the inside scoop.

"So, Beez, I've got some municipal bonds, and I've got some other investments, land, stocks and whatnot, but the bonds have got coupons. I clip the coupons, drop 'em off or send 'em in and you guys send me a check." Hawkins said. "These are different you say. How so?"

"Well, they're sold at a discount to face value. Redeemed at face value in three years, five years, ten years." Beasley explained. "This just started. It's pretty neat. The bonds in circulation are mostly bought by banks and the big dollar investors. Brokerage houses. Not your mom and pops."

"Interesting, Beez. So, no coupons? Nothing to clip? Buy 'em at less than face value, redeem 'em at face value?"

Beasley nodded.

"And this just started?"

"Yeah, the legislature just passed a bill creating the program. They also created a sinking fund to cover debt service. Well, kind of a sinking fund. It's a debt-service fund. Used to pay the redemptions. It's made up of a portion of the bond sales and a dedicated portion of the new income tax receipts. Excess cash over what's needed for redemption is used for early redemption," Beasley explained to the clearly interested Hawkins.

"Why they doing this, Beez?"

"That's the neat part, Gabe. They're using the rest of the proceeds for what they call 'flood control projects,' but they're really just big fishing lakes. Put people to work building the lakes." Beasley was on a roll. "There's even talk of tweaking the law next time the legislature meets so the state can sell off land for cabins, boat docks, retail, things like that. Bring in a few more bucks."

The wheels were turning fiercely in Gabe Hawkins' well-oiled brain. "So, you see the bonds? You touch 'em?"

"I have dreams about these bonds, Gabe," Beasley said, feigning boredom. "My goodness, right now it's a big part of what I do. Almost all I'm doing these days. It was a four-mil issue!"

"Get outta here!" Hawkins exclaimed. "My goodness." Hawkins thought for a moment. "So, Beez, who else touches these bonds? Who handles 'em? Besides you."

Beasley pondered for a couple seconds. "Well, there's me, the State Auditor signs 'em, the State Treasurer signs 'em, bond counsel from Wichita, there's a brokerage house in KC that's bought some, a couple big ones in New York, one or two in Chicago . . . oh yeah, a number of banks throughout the state. Mostly bigger ones, but some small ones, too." Beasley felt the need to share the detailed, dreary information that would surely uninvite him to future dinner parties. "The banks buy 'em and then turn around and use 'em as security for deposits of State dollars."

"Okay," Beasley added, "you're gonna think I'm weird, but I know all their signatures by heart. I can do 'em all."

"I'm sorry," Hawkins looked over the top of his drink glass, "you lost me there. Whadda ya mean you know 'em by heart? What's that mean?"

Beasley searched his pockets and pulled out his pen and a folded piece of paper. He unfolded it, checked the printed side, turned it over to the blank side and quickly scribbled two signatures. He rotated the paper for Hawkins to see, then pointed at one of the signatures. "The Treasurer's signature." He pointed at the other. "That's the Auditor's signature." He looked intently at Hawkins. "You could compare those to the real ones and I guarantee you can't tell the difference."

As all of this was sinking in with Hawkins, Beasley rotated the paper again and produced a distinctive flurry of loops that Hawkins recognized right away, even upside down. "Oh my God, Beez. That's mine." Hawkins looked up from the paper at Beasley. "You're incredible. How in the world . . . ?"

Beasley sheepishly described a lonely boy with few friends, and sometimes no friends at all, a framed copy of the Declaration of Independence received on his eighth birthday, fascination with John Hancock's flowing signature, a healthy helping of obsessive behavior, and the rest was history.

"Geez, I'm sorry, Beez, but you gotta know you've got a real talent here." Hawkins felt like adding he knew people who might pay for a talent like this, but figured he'd best keep it to himself for the time being.

Hawkins fired off questions about face value of the bonds, maturities, the KC brokerage, how much was sitting in the Treasurer's vault, how much was out in circulation. He looked at his watch. "Beez, I gotta run. Your old man's not gonna be happy if I'm late." He paused. "Say, let's do lunch again. Soon. Oh yeah, you okay if I take your signatures?" Beasley nodded as Hawkins folded up the paper and put it in his shirt pocket.

"Of course, Gabe. Lunch is on me next time."

Two months later Hawkins called again. "I'll pick up some sodas and sandwiches, Beez, and pick you up at home after work. Where do ya live?"

That evening the two friends drove to Gage Park on the west edge of Topeka and found a picnic table in the shade. "Don't say a word 'til I'm done, Beez. Just hear me out."

As Beasley ate, the businesslike Hawkins laid out the scheme, telling Beasley what he needed to know, but nothing he didn't need to know. Hawkins didn't share he'd purchased one of the State's new bonds and he'd reached out to a friend in the mob, describing a fool-proof plan to make 'em all rich. He didn't share with Beasley how he'd met with the mobster, showing him the State bond and Beasley's fake signatures. He didn't share the mob would take care of the forged bonds and laundering 'em through a Chicago brokerage house. They just needed Beasley to sign the bonds. That was it.

"We do this in five, six runs," Hawkins added. "A couple hundred thousand per, maybe three hundred thousand. Nothin's set in stone. Serial numbers of those in circulation and those out of circulation. Mix it up." Hawkins looked at his friend. "Whadda ya think, Beez?"

Beasley had finished his sandwich. He downed the rest of his soda. "No."

Hawkins waited for more. Beasley looked up from the table. Their eyes met. "No?" Hawkins asked. "No way at all? You sure?"

Beasley shook his head slowly. "No way at all."

"Hmm. Almost forgot to tell you, Beez," Hawkins added, "but there's cash up front for us. Thirty percent of face value. We split it. We promise to deliver a hundred thou and you get fifteen, I get fifteen. You can buy a really nice house and a really nice car for that amount. And, you've got cash left over."

Hawkins looked at Beasley. He's listening, Hawkins thought. "We do one, two mil over the next year and you never have to work again." Hawkins paused. "Whadda ya think, Beez?"

"What about prison?"

He's not a 'no,' Hawkins thought. "I'm glad you asked that question, Beez. So, do I look like someone who wants to spend twenty years in the clink? Huh?"

Beasley stopped short. "Okay, how do we get away with it? Why do the bonds in circulation? Why not just those in the vault?"

"Think about it, Beez. If we use bonds in and out of circulation, it'll dilute the focus. Everyone's a suspect. The bonds will be a perfect match, so you got the printer, the people who work at the printer. Bond counsel. The Treasurer. The Auditor."

"And me," Beasley added.

"Yes," Hawkins agreed, "you'd be a suspect, too, but less so than if we just use the serial numbers of those sitting five feet away from ya. Know what I mean?" Hawkins watched as Beasley nodded in recognition. "Look, at some point this is gonna fall apart. No question about it. Someone'll figure it out, and then it all comes tumblin' down. That is absolutely gonna occur." Hawkins paused, holding up his forefinger. "But the law doesn't charge what the law can't prove, and those doin' the investigatin' ain't the brightest bulbs in the box."

Hawkins let his words of wisdom sink in. "Here's all you gotta do, Beez ..." Hawkins emphasized the need to hide the blank bonds, to work at night with shades drawn. Don't say anything. Never admit anything. Deny everything. None of the cash could be spent, deposited or invested. "Bury it if you need to," Hawkins said. "Someday it's yours to spend, but not now or anytime soon."

Hawkins threw out a plan for the two to hook up on a regular basis. "Whadda ya think, Beez? We need ya. This doesn't happen without ya."

"I'll let you know," Beasley said, knowing there was no way he was going to sign on to a hare-brained plot sure to land him in a Lansing prison cell.

"You're gonna be a rich man. Beez. Beyond your wildest dreams. Oh yeah," Hawkins added, "I'll need serial number sequences, denominations and redemption dates." Hawkins, ever the closer, shifted gears. "Beez, how'd your daddy pay for that new Packard? Huh?"

Beasley weighed the question, but didn't respond.

Hawkins continued. "Well, it wasn't from selling life insurance, that's for sure. And you know it. That business is dead meat right now. Am I right?"

Beasley acknowledged that, yes, his father had to let the young widow go, as well as the part-time girl, but his long-time aide, Mrs. Ames, still held down a job. Barely, he figured.

"Think about it, Beez. Yup, your old man makes dough right here in Topeka, helping people like me get things done. That new Packard paid for our changes to the business inventory law."

Beasley ran it through his head, not wanting to believe what his friend was telling him, but knowing it might be true.

"It's how business gets done, Beez," Hawkins added. "Your daddy's a good man. Gave people jobs, provided for his family. He's a success 'cause he can play the game. He gets it." Hawkins turned and laid a gentle hand on Beasley's shoulder. "Look, Beez, sooner or later you'll get it, too. It'll click for ya. May as well be now when the gettin's good."

The two men got up from the park bench and started toward Hawkins' polished Ford. Beasley stopped and looked at the expensive car. "I'll think about it, Gabe. I'll let you know."

# WEST BOTTOMS

## SUMMER 1933, THE SCHEME COMES TOGETHER

Beasley laid motionless on his back atop the thin white sheet of his boardinghouse bed. Another droplet of sweat formed within the forest of hair and, like a cautious bunny hopping from tree trunk to tree trunk, rolled haltingly downhill from hair to hair. He fought the screaming urge to scratch his head, make the ticklish sensation stop, but found the bead of sweat a welcome distraction to frustrating indecision over Hawkins' proposal, the crushing thought his father was taking bribes, and the very real prospect of years in a stank Lansing cell, sharing lice-infested bunks with a hulking, tattooed lifer.

Out the open window of his humble second-floor room the faint glow of dawn signaled the beginning of yet another brutally hot, cloudless summer day. Beasley had slept fitfully at best. Throughout the night he'd examined every life path Hawkins' proposal might take him, yet hours later he was no closer to knowing an answer. What he should tell his friend was easy. 'No. Hell no.' He kept circling back to the 'buts,' finding himself rationalizing a choice he knew was wrong. Maybe his father had wrestled with similar thoughts once upon a time? Surely not now, he figured.

What would he tell his friend? He didn't know.

Not four blocks away from Beasley's low-rent boarding house and a mere three blocks west of the State Capitol building, Elwood Sneed examined his teeth in the mirror of the widow Thompson's upstairs bathroom. The meticulous, never-married, always serious chief of staff to the Kansas State Treasurer's minimal, hard-working staff rubbed a dab of hair cream in the palms of his hands, then ran both across his thinning hair. After carefully combing his neatly cropped hair, insuring not a strand was out of place, he finished with a perfectly straight part.

Elwood leaned toward the mirror and checked his teeth a final time, then tightened the knot of his tie, slid into his suit coat and headed downstairs where the plump, equally serious Widow Thompson stood waiting with Elwood's brown-bag lunch and umbrella. Elwood nodded his thanks, stepped out onto the porch and started his brisk walk to the office where he'd served six state treasurers over thirty-three years.

A non-political bureaucrat, Elwood was the consummate survivor. Competent, incredibly discrete and unflinchingly loyal to the latest office leader, one elected treasurer after another had quickly learned retaining the meticulous Sneed was a better proposition to removing him with uncertain results. Today, however, would be a bit of a test for Sneed.

A little more than a mile south of downtown, State Treasurer Norman Pfister stood at the dining room window of his comfortable, well-appointed Quinton Heights home watching two squirrels playfully chase one another around the trunk of a backyard tree. He took a last sip of coffee before turning to Grace, his high school sweetheart and wife of forty years, giving her a peck on the cheek. "We'll drive out to Hays this weekend," he told her. He held up his leather briefcase. "The contracts and deeds are ready. Read all of it last night. Twice. Time to get this done."

Pfister and his wife saw light at the end of the tunnel. Retirement, travel and never working again was in sight. At the end of this, his fifth two-year term, the two would sell the Topeka home, grab their bags and sail to Athens, the start of a three-month tour of the holy land and Europe, culminating with two weeks in Paris. Grace couldn't wait. Pfister couldn't wait to give Grace her lifelong dream of visiting the ancient sites, immersing herself in the old-world culture she'd dreamed of experiencing since she was a schoolgirl in pigtails milking the family cow.

Pfister's mind drifted as his Ford cruised toward downtown. The bank in Hays would be sold to the couple's eldest son, the bank in Russell to their younger son, and the thousand-acre ranch and cattle herd would go to their daughter and son-in-law. The future stream of income would more than adequately fund the couple's golden years at their small mountain ranch in the Rockies above Boulder. More and more Pfister imagined starry sky nights on his log cabin deck, studying the moon and planets with his latest and greatest telescope, a life-long passion short-circuited when, as a student at the University of Kansas, he was suddenly called home to Hays to take over as bank president following the unexpected passing of his father. The role of State Treasurer had been another unexpected fork-in-the-road turn he reluctantly accepted eight years earlier when the incumbent died at his desk and the governor reached out to Pfister, a non-politician, a banker, to complete the dead man's term. Four elections later Pfister was ready to call it quits.

First, though, Pfister needed to deal with the current governor's latest political stunt. Well, maybe it wasn't totally a stunt. Times were tough on a good number of people, after all, but the Governor's directive all agencies cut spending by ten percent was going to hit his small staff hard. First on the agenda that morning would be to hear Elwood Sneed's ideas on how to achieve the ten-percent cut, a task he'd assigned late the day before following the governor's widely attended news conference.

Sneed closed his office door and composed himself. He checked his teeth and hair in the small mirror on the wall, grabbed his notepad and headed down the hall to the Treasurer's office. The door was open. Pfister waved him in. "Shut the door, Elwood. Please."

Sneed took a seat across the solid oak desk from the business-like Pfister. "So, what're you thinking Elwood? How do we make this work?"

Each man, for his own reasons, was concerned the impact a cut in pay might have on the small office staff. Except for the recently hired Beasley Wentsworth, a political favor hire if ever there was one, each of the staff was a woman, several of whom were widows or older, or both. Each man knew a ten-percent cut in pay would hit the ladies hard.

Sneed looked at his notes, sucked in a breath and got straight to the point. "If we eliminate Wentsworth's position and you and I take a three percent cut in pay, cut back on this and that, we'll finish the fiscal year within the governor's directive."

Sneed looked up at Pfister for a sign on how his proposal was received. He'd heard the scuttlebutt surrounding Beasley's hiring, that Pfister's arm was twisted by the governor to make the hire to nail down support from Beasley's father, the powerful Ways and Means Committee chairman, on a rural electrification bill. It worked; the bill passed. Sneed, however, didn't like the hire, and was more than a little resentful at having the young Wentsworth forced on him. Sneed bit his tongue, though, kept his thoughts to himself, smiled and did his job. The ultimate survivor. Sneed stuck the unaware Beasley at a desk in the cramped, stuffy Treasurer's vault, separated from the rest of the staff.

Pfister leaned back in his chair, reflecting on the proposal. The pay cut wasn't an issue for him and the populist in him wanted the ladies to be left whole. Firing young Wentsworth wouldn't go over well, but Pfister didn't care. He was sure the senator was corrupt as they come, and the governor was just another cookie-cutter political insider, a climber. Besides, he and Grace would be forever finished with the political drama nonsense in a matter of months.

"Thank you, Elwood. Do it. And I'll eat the salary cuts."

Sneed nodded and stood up. Pfister held up his hand. "Elwood, give young Wentsworth through the end of the week. Tell him straight away. I'll call the senator in a few minutes."

Sneed left, closing the door behind him. He was elated, not so much that his loyal staff would be left unharmed by the governor's cut, or that the Treasurer trusted him and accepted his proposal, but that he'd be the one to tell the privileged rich kid to hit the pavement.

Sneed bypassed his office and headed straight to the vault. A tired, slightly unkempt Beasley looked up from a stack of bonds. Sneed cut straight to the chase. "Effective end of the day on Friday your position will be eliminated due to the Governor's ten-percent cut. State-issued property should be left on your desk before leaving."

Sneed turned sharply and left before the dumb-struck Beasley could say a word. He pushed back his chair and hustled out of the vault, catching up to Sneed as he reached his office door. Sneed turned in the doorway and faced

Beasley. "Make sure to leave behind all State-issued property." With that Sneed shut the door behind him, leaving Beasley speechless.

Head down, Beasley walked slowly back to the vault and plopped down in his chair. He stared blankly at the stack of bonds. He picked up his phone and placed a call. "Gabe, this is Beasley. I'm in."

# WEST BOTTOMS

# SUNDAY, JULY 8, 1934, MORNING

Angelo "The Fist" Ricitti buttoned his jacket and walked up the steps to the front door of an unassuming brick home in a tree-lined Cicero, Illinois neighborhood, removing his fedora before knocking. A tiny woman with a Mona Lisa smile and salt-and- pepper hair pulled tightly into a bun, answered the door, beckoning the capo in and leading him to the rear of the home.

"He's on the back porch with his coffee and the Tribune," she said, opening the door to the covered porch.

Chicago Outfit boss Tony "Big Whale" Bunicci, not expecting company on a Sunday morning and dressed only in his bathrobe and leather slippers, removed his reading glasses and stood to greet the younger man, one he'd mentored since the trusted capo was barely into his teens.

"Please have a seat Angelo," Bunicci said as the two men eased into matching wicker chairs. "It is always good to see you."

It had been eight months since Ricitti last walked the creaky wood floors of the house in which he'd spent so many hours as a teenager, effectively an adopted older brother to the Bunicci boys–Simon, Lucas, Peter and Paul. Simon, the oldest, wasn't inclined toward loansharking or rum-running and had left for Paris years before when he was barely out of his teens. Over the succeeding years Simon had created a unique niche for himself in the world of fine art, where his far-ranging list of contacts and discretion as a curator of art by the masters was in demand from an elite clientele across Europe, Asia and North America.

The ever-physical, rambunctious twins, Lucas and Peter, had clamored to follow their father into the Outfit. Each made capo shortly after their father ascended to Outfit boss during the somewhat uncertain and tumultuous period following the October 1931 tax evasion conviction of Big Al Capone. The family's baby boy, Paul, was a mix of his older brothers: the calm, considered intellect of Simon, and the inborn fearlessness of the twins.

43

His father's favorite, the diminutive Paul was but three years removed from a degree in Western History from Harvard. Despite his smaller stature, the twins stopped picking on their little brother about the time he reached puberty and started punching back. Of course, in a real fight - a knock-down, drag-out fight - the twins' younger brother wouldn't stand a chance against either of them, let alone both, but even at this early age it was clear little Paul would rather be beaten into submission than to stop swinging and kicking. Little Paulie earned their respect.

The last time Ricitti had joined his adopted family was the evening of December 6, 1933. The table in the small dining room was completely covered with plates, the remnants of bread loaves, empty wine bottles, and several large porcelain bowls which, only thirty minutes earlier, had been heaping full of meatballs, steaming pasta and Sicilian red sauce.

The walls of the Bunicci home barely contained the jubilant conversation, the unrestrained voices stepping all over each other, the exuberance of the Bunicci clan. Lucas returned from the kitchen with another bottle of wine, popped the cork and quickly drained it, refilling the heirloom lead crystal wine glasses about the table, glasses that arrived from the old country on a cramped, smelly steamship, each wrapped in bed clothing and carefully packed in a small box. Mrs. Bunicci brought these glasses out only for the most special occasions, and adoption of the 21st amendment repealing prohibition the day before was deemed by her husband to be just such an occasion.

Tony reached over and squeezed his wife's hand, giving her a quick smile before pushing away from the table and walking to his study, closing the door behind him. She leaned over to her youngest boy and said quietly, "Paulie, go join your father in his study. He's waiting for you."

Paul thought the request a bit odd but nodded his head and left to join his father. Opening the study door Paul found his father behind his desk, hunched over the small fireplace hearth with a fire poker in one hand, adding kindling to the glowing embers with the other. He turned and motioned his son to a padded armchair close to the growing flames, turning further as

Lucas stepped into the study with an armful of additional firewood. "Thank you, Luke. Please set it here by the hearth."

The twin carefully laid the dry wood where instructed, then winked and shot a smile to Paul as he stood to leave.

"Please shut the door behind you, Luke," Tony instructed. "My best to your lovely wife and children."

The elder Bunicci placed several small pieces of split wood on the fire, poked it all a couple more times, then stood slowly, stretching his back. He smiled at his youngest son. "Can't fight age, Paulie. I'm not getting younger. Neither is your mother."

Tony stepped by his youngest son and sat in the study's other padded armchair. "Change is upon us, Paulie. Many don't wanna see it, but it's here, and the old days are gone. They're not coming back."

Paul didn't necessarily disagree with the 'change is coming' commentary, snippets of which he'd heard in hushed conversations over the past year or so.

"Paulie, several years ago one of our friends warned me never to get between a reporter and the Big Guy. The man loved being in the newspapers. He craved attention." Tony tapped his temple with a bony forefinger. "Not smart. Not with what we do. And he's a real hot-head, brutal when it wasn't needed. He ruled with terror, not from the respect and loyalty of his people. Again, not smart. We shoot up people with Tommy guns, massacres, gun battles in the streets, blood stains on city sidewalks. Taunting the government. We're inviting heat. Not good, Paulie."

Tony studied his son's face. Paul was listening intently, knowing this, the intimate one-on-one in his father's small study, the direct critique of Capone, which was new and unexpected, all of it, was going somewhere important.

"So, there's incredible opportunity if we stop poking the bear and embrace our changing America. The shop owner who's scraping by, he doesn't care what we do, until he does. Now he cares, because he reads the papers. Dead bodies sell newspapers. Gang wars sell newspapers. Scaring your neighbors sells newspapers." Tony stood, stepped over and stirred the fire with the poker. "When people get scared they look to the politicians, and the politicians panic, pressuring the coppers. The coppers put the squeeze on us. Questions, Paulie?"

Paul shook his head.

Tony continued. "It wasn't just the Big Guy. New York, too. Now, the feds have geared up really big and really fast, and they're a real threat if we don't change. We need new leaders, smart guys that get it. We do that, we'll be okay."

"That's you, pops," Paul said.

Tony smiled. "Maybe so, Paulie, but I'm old, ready to be done, take your mother to Florida where it never snows. Sit on the beach all day with my lemonade. Capisce?"

"I do, pops."

"Good, good. See, Paulie, we've cleaned things up. We've got a truce with the Irish. Boundaries. They make money, we make money. No one wins with wars, killing each other. There's plenty for everyone if we don't mess it up."

"Now, Paulie," Tony continued, "it's time for us to evolve. Faster. Respectable stuff that makes a lot of money. Not just the trash business, the salvage yards. Real business. Trucking. Shipping. Booze. Legit."

Paul raised a hand. "But, what about – "

Tony interrupted his son. "That doesn't change, Paulie. The guy on a barstool still wants to place a bet. He still wants to have a roll before going home to the missus. What changes is what we do with our earnings, and what we do with each other. No more wars. No more celebrity bosses posing for the press. If the guy on the barstool knows my name, I'm doing it all wrong. Our friends in New York agree."

Tony paused and looked intently at his youngest son. "We do this by having the right leaders. Leaders with vision for what we can be, where we can be." He paused again. "You, Paulie. We need you."

Paul sat back, stunned. He wasn't expecting this. Not at all. He knew the one-on-one with his father was something of consequence, but not this.

Not in his wildest dreams.

Paul let it sink in before speaking. "What about Luke and Petie? They're capos."

The elder Bunicci laughed. "It was their idea!"

"What about Angelo?" Paul asked. The Fist was like another big brother, but he was different, too. He had an edge, a ruthlessness even the twins were cautious not to unleash. "Have you talked to him?"

"No, Paulie, Angelo doesn't know," Tony said. "He mustn't know." Tony had wrestled with this decision for some time. No, not the transfer of power to Paul. That made total sense. The twins saw it before him, but once they brought the idea to him, it was like he'd discovered the nose on his face. It was unbelievably obvious. What to do about Ricitti, though, wasn't obvious at all.

"I don't think Angelo's gonna like it," Paul said, now growing a bit concerned. "What about his crew?"

"Don't worry about Angelo's crew, Paulie," Tony said. "They're loyal to him 'cause they're afraid of him, not because they respect him. A lot more fear than respect. They'll be fine."

"So, what's the plan with Angelo, pops?"

Tony smiled, leaned forward and patted Paul's leg. "I'm still reflecting. It'll come to me."

Tony stood and started toward the study door. Paul followed. "One more thing, Paulie. Remember this word: Eureka. You may never hear it again, but if you do it means you can trust the person saying it. Okay?"

Paul nodded. "Eureka. Okay, pops."

Now, eight months since that celebratory, cold December night, Ricitti had serious business to discuss with the boss.

"Tony, we may have a – " Ricitti stopped mid-sentence as the older man raised a finger to his mouth.

"I'm sorry, Angelo," Bunicci said with a knowing smile, "but please wait just a moment." No sooner had he finished but his wife opened the door to the porch, a steaming cup of coffee in hand for the unexpected guest. Having provided for their guest, Mrs. Bunicci turned and, without a word, retreated into the couple's home.

Bunicci smiled again. "After a while, my friend, we learn each other's habits. See, my beloved wife is from the old country. To not show courtesy to our guest would bring dishonor to the family." Bunicci leaned back and crossed his legs. "She will not be back, Angelo." Bunicci motioned with his hand for Ricitti to speak.

"We may have a problem, Tony," Ricitti said as he leaned forward, lowering his voice. "Our boy in Kansas City didn't meet me at Union Station last night. I was last to board and he never showed. I got back here less than an hour ago. Our package is missing."

Bunicci rubbed his chin. "And we're sure our boy had a package to deliver?"

"Yes, Tony. He called Sal on Thursday, telling Sal that he's 'anxious to see Chicago.' Our meet is always on a Saturday night following his call, there at the station in KC. Three calls, three deliveries." Ricitti continued. "It could be a flat tire, Tony. It could be nothin'. But I stopped by Sal's home on my way here and Sal's heard nothin' since Thursday. My gut tells me we may have a problem. Our boy in KC has our thirty grand, Tony. He's got the package. Think he's double-crossin' us?"

"I don't know, Angelo. Could be." Bunicci considered the situation for a moment. "Okay, Angelo, go get Paulie and get him on the train this afternoon." Bunicci ripped off a corner of the Tribune front page and scribbled a telephone number on it. "Have Sal call this number and tell him to talk to Tommy Lozarro in Kansas City. No one else. Only Tommy." He handed the number to Ricitti. "Tell Sal to ask Tommy if he'll send one of his guys to meet Paulie at the station, drive him around."

Tony continued. "Tommy'll do me a favor. And, Angelo, fill in Paulie and let him know we just want the package. Just find the package and bring it home."

He paused again. "But, and tell him this, too, if this thing is unraveling we're going to need to clean up the loose ends. Roll it up. He may need to find out who's signing the bonds. Tell him to communicate through Sal, but only as needed."

Ricitti nodded. "Done. But, Tony, you sure you wanna send Paulie?"

"He's my son, Angelo. I trust him like I trust you. This is what he wants. He's ready."

After Ricitti left Bunicci got up from his chair and walked slowly into the house, deep in thought. Down the hall and across from the small dining room he opened the door to his study and took a seat at his mahogany desk. Opening a drawer, he fished around until he found the scrap of paper with a name and number and placed a call. "This is Tony Bunicci. We spoke about a mutually beneficial project some time ago."

"Two hours. Grant Park, take a bench at Buckingham Fountain. I'll find ya," said the gruff voice on the other end of the call.

# WEST BOTTOMS

# MONDAY, JULY 9, 1934, MORNING

$A$s was generally the case, Kansas City, Kansas detective Mark Diehl had reached his desk in the department's squad room before anyone else. He stared down at the thin manila case file that rested in the center of his desk, uncluttered save for the framed picture of his little sister. He stripped off his suit coat and dropped it across the back of his wood banker's chair, loosened his tie, unbuttoned the top button of his pressed dress shirt, turned on his desk lamp and flipped open the case file.

One page. Just a criminal complaint form completed by someone. No initials. No time. Victim by the name of Gabriel Hawkins. No assault, no weapon, no perp description. Diehl knew that fancy name from somewhere but was clueless why he'd been pegged to investigate a simple car theft.

Detective Tim Brandt hacked up some phlegm as he shuffled into the squad room, an unlit cigarette hanging from his lips. He stopped at the coffee pot near his desk. Diehl held up the file and shouted to him. "Hey, Brandt, you leave this on my desk?"

Brandt paused and looked at Diehl. "Nope."

"It's a car theft, Brandt. More your speed, I'd think."

Brandt plopped down at his desk, ignoring the sleight.

My God, Diehl thought. How does a knuckle-dragging, St. Louis flatfoot slob like Brandt make detective here in KC?

"Diehl!" Captain John Mulroney's voice filled the mostly empty squad room. The squad's leader was punctual, as usual. Most days he walked in at 7:15 a.m., as he did this morning. "We need to talk."

Diehl rolled back from his desk, stood up and followed the captain to his corner office. "Close the door and do the blinds for me, will ya, Diehl? And have a seat." Mulroney fired up a short, fat cigar as Diehl sat down across the desk from him.

Mulroney tolerated the tall, athletic Diehl. Actually, respected him might be a better way to describe how he felt about the college boy who'd made detective in short order after joining the force, and was clearly born for something greater than busting up gambling rings, but seemed in no hurry to get there.

"You're wondering about the car theft?"

Diehl nodded.

"It's an odd duck, Diehl." Mulroney leaned back in his chair and eyed the young detective. "So, yesterday morning, pretty fuckin' early mind you, I get a call from the Chief. Hadn't even had time to take a shit. Well, the Chief tells me he's just got off the phone with the Mayor."

Mulroney paused, knocked the ash from his cigar and re-lit it, the end glowing red again after a couple of quick sucks. Diehl sat motionless, waiting for the rest of story.

"So, the Mayor knows this Hawkins guy. Actually, the Mayor kinda knows him, but he's a real close friend with this twit's big shot dad." Mulroney shot a glance toward his office door and waved someone away.

"Old man Hawkins owns Hawkins Sand and Gravel, a trucking company, a lumber yard, and a bunch of other shit. Big-time involved in the plaza area development. Makes more in a day than we make in a year. Know what I mean, Diehl?"

"Yeah, he's in the room while we're cooling our heels on the sidewalk." Diehl said, not unaware of the special attention paid to those in power, and those who put them in power.

"You've got the picture, Diehl."

Mulroney continued. "Well, the Mayor tells the Chief his buddy's son has his pretty green Ford Model A stolen from outside the River City sometime on Saturday night. Maybe early Sunday morning. Apparently, it's one of the twit's favorite watering holes."

Diehl spoke up. "The Mayor gets a call from this guy's rich daddy over a stolen car? He could buy another with the loose change in his pocket."

"Right, right, but that's just a piece of it, Diehl." Mulroney knocked some ash from the cigar and dropped it in the ashtray. "Get this, Diehl. The Chief didn't wanna tell me the twit's name. And get this. He wanted me to type up a complaint using a fake name for the victim. Doesn't want this guy's name on the complaint."

Diehl furrowed a brow. "Hmm. That's interesting."

"Exactly. And I'm thinking 'what the fuck.' I told him 'fuck it, Harold, you type up the complaint.' He got a little huffy with that," Mulroney chuckled.

"So, I tell him, 'Okay, I'll type it up, but I'm using your name.'" Mulroney laughed, shaking his head. "Man, you'd think I put a gun to his head. He exploded, started spittin' and stammerin'. And, that's when he gives me the twit's name, orders me to find the car chop-chop, and hangs up on me."

Mulroney leaned back and looked at Diehl. "So, now you know what I know. Questions?"

"Yeah, why me?"

"You're my best ID, Diehl. Hands down. Find me the car, okay. But a word to the wise, Diehl." Mulroney leaned forward and lowered his voice. "I think ya need to work alone, and I think ya need to watch your back. Only talk to me about this one. There's a bit of a stench to it. Know what I mean, Diehl?" For his own reasons, Mulroney didn't mention the Chief's order Diehl be given the case.

Diehl nodded. He wasn't totally sure he was on the same page, but the vote of confidence felt good. "This'll be a nice little challenge, Cap. I'll find the car."

Diehl headed to his desk across a now-bustling squad room. "Hey Diehl, your sister called."

Diehl eased down into his chair, his mind racing way ahead of the limited facts available to him. He knew to be a good detective, to be good at anything in life for that matter, he needed to return to his lodestar: discipline, be methodical, facts, facts, facts, A to B to C.

Diehl picked up the receiver and dialed his sister's number. She answered after the first ring. "This is Lulu." Diehl smiled. He couldn't help it. Lulu was his kid sister, four years younger, always positive, cheerful, but strong as Atlas inside. Heaven help the arrogant fool who might take her kindness for weakness, he thought.

"Hey, dumbass, what's up." His smile widened.

"Dumbass?" Lulu feigned indignation. "I should knock your block off you... donkey poop." They both laughed. As long as each could remember she was "dumbass" and he was "donkey poop," the best response in the moment a four-year old Lulu could come up with when her revered big brother made her cry. It stuck.

"Okay, kiddo, what's up. I've stepped in a bucket here. Gotta keep movin'."

"Hmm, something interesting?"

"Can't talk about it, kiddo."

"Okaaay, Mr. Big Shot police man. Sooo, how 'bout drinks this evening? On me. We need to celebrate."

"Celebrate?"

"I got a gig!" Lulu shouted with glee. "Jacob, Mr. Greenberg, at the Morpheum, is giving me five minutes before The Catskills touring show in a couple weeks. It's my big break, donkey poop!"

"Wow, this is exciting, kiddo." Diehl got serious. He knew how hard his little sister had worked to break into Vaudeville. This was her dream. Always had been. Yeah, during the day she toiled at Macy's selling panties and other unspeakables to the rich ladies who looked down on her, but she had her dreams, and making those dreams come true in Kansas City, of all places, wasn't easy.

Diehl delivered the set-up line. "Goodness, what lovely diamonds you have . . . dumbass."

"Goodness had nothing to do with it . . . donkey poop."

If he hadn't known better Diehl would've thought he was talking to the sultry Mae West.

Lulu continued. "Hang on, hang on, check this out and tell me who it is," followed by a spot-on impersonation of the irrepressible new first lady, Eleanor Roosevelt.

# WEST BOTTOMS

## MONDAY, JULY 9, 1934, EVENING

It was dusk when Diehl turned west onto a deserted Guilford Lane and let his unmarked Studebaker Commander idle forward close to the curb until he was across from the Mission Hills home of Gabriel Hawkins. It takes some greenbacks to live in an exclusive neighborhood like this, Diehl thought as he killed the headlights and engine, and gave the expansive Tudor set well back from the street a quick once-over. The detached three-car garage with living quarters above was twice the size of his comfortable but modest bungalow. Quarters above the garage, Diehl thought. If nothing else, he's likely got a maid.

Diehl pulled a notepad from his breast pocket and flipped it open, thumbing the pages until he came to Hawkins' scribbled address. He glanced back at the house to confirm the street number. Except for burning lamps on either side of the front door, the house was dark.

Diehl opened the car door, halting to avoid stepping in front of a Ford that passed by from behind. Safe to cross the street Diehl made his way up the long, stone walkway to the front door and, with the large brass knocker, announced his presence. He swayed back and forth as he waited in front of the solid wood door. Nothing. He knocked again and waited. Still nothing.

"Don't stop, Vinny. Keep on going." Paul Bunicci said to Vincenzo "Mad Dog" Grazoni, a local made man acting as chauffeur and muscle, a favor paid to Paul's father.

Vinny accelerated and the Ford drove past Diehl as he was stepping out of the Studebaker in front of Hawkins' house. Paul turned in his seat and looked back at the man who'd exited the Studebaker and was crossing the street toward Hawkins' home. "Let's circle around and park back where we can see what this guy's doing."

"Is that your boy?" Vinny asked.

"Hawkins would've parked up by his house." Paul said. "I'm guessin' that guy's a copper, Vinny. Recognize him?"

Vinny shook his head. "I've gotta few guys on the Kansas side, but I've never seen him. I'll make a call later."

Vinny killed the lights and slowed the Ford as they approached the rear of Diehl's Studebaker, stopping well back. Hawkins' house was dark and they couldn't see the copper. Vinny reached into his breast pocket and pulled out a pack of Lucky Strikes, offering one to Paul, who shook his head. Vinny struck a match and fired up a cigarette, taking a deep draw.

Diehl stepped back from the entryway and carefully checked each of the windows along the front of the house. Drapes drawn, no lights, no movement. He strolled along the front of the house to the driveway, checking the garage and side of the house for any sign of life. Nothing. He walked up the drive and peered into the back yard. Nothing.

Assuming no one was home, Diehl headed back down the drive to his car.

Paul pointed. "Here he comes, Vinny. That didn't take long."

"The house looks empty." Vinny said.

"Could be, but we need to check anyway. Never know."

As he opened the car door Diehl noticed the Ford parked half a block behind his Studebaker. Pretending not to notice the Ford, Diehl slid in behind the wheel and adjusted the rearview mirror. There it is, he smiled, the faint glow of a lit cigarette. Driver's seat. He pulled forward and motored to the next corner, where he turned left and was soon out of sight.

Paul and Vinny watched in silence as Diehl drove off, waiting until the car was out of sight before slowly pulling forward across from Hawkins' home. Vinny flicked the cigarette out onto the street and the two exited the Ford, walking quickly across the street and up the long drive. "I'll check the front, Vinny. Head around back and see if a door's unlocked."

Paul knocked on the front door. No answer. He tried the door handle, but the door was locked. He stepped back from the entryway and checked the front of the house. No movement and all the shades were drawn.

Meanwhile, after leaving Hawkins' house, Diehl looped back around to Guilford Lane. Retracing his earlier route, Diehl soon saw the Ford, parked maybe a block ahead across from Hawkins' house. Diehl cut his lights and engine, and coasted to a stop along the curb. He grabbed his binoculars off the passenger seat and adjusted the magnification until he could read the Ford's license plate: 216 dash 545. Diehl scribbled down the plate number, then scanned the car and what he could see of the front of Hawkins' home. No signs of life. Best he could tell the car's occupants had exited, but where they'd gone, he had no idea.

That mystery didn't last long.

As Paul reached the driveway he was stopped dead in his tracks by a woman's scream from the back of the house. Before he could take another step Vinny came flying around a backside corner of the house, his unbuttoned suit coat flapping behind him.

"Go, go, go!" Vinny shouted as he waved toward the car. Paul wheeled around and started running down the drive, quickly caught by a surprisingly fleet Vinny, a hulking middle-aged man with the body of a Northwest logger.

The two reached the Ford at full speed, Paul still unsure why they were fleeing the scene. Vinny didn't pause to explain. He fired up the Ford and hit the gas.

"What happened, Vinny?"

Vinny stared straight ahead, intent on making the turns that would get them back to the Missouri state line in the shortest distance.

"The fuckin' old bitch had a double-barrel. Six inches from my chest." Vinny was clearly unnerved, still staring straight ahead.

"Who was she, Vinny?" Paul asked calmly as Vinny took a curve a little too fast, the Ford's rear end skidding before straightening out again.

"Dunno. A little dame. Short hair. Hmm, maybe a maid. I think she was wearin' maid get-up. I only saw her for a second."

No sooner had Diehl set the binoculars back on the seat than he heard the shrill scream that pierced the quiet summer eve. Almost immediately he observed two dark figures running pall mall down Hawkins' driveway before jumping into the Ford. The car's tires screeched as the driver floored it, hurrying down the street and quickly out of sight.

After seeing the commotion, Diehl started the Studebaker and rushed up to Hawkins' home. He ran up the drive to the back of the house, turning the home's corner to find a petite, middle-age woman standing outside near an open door, gripping a double-barrel shotgun with both hands. The old woman wheeled on Diehl as he skidded to a halt and threw up both arms.

"Police! Police! Don't shoot!" Diehl shouted instinctively.

For a split-second Diehl thought he was a dead man, but then the tension in the old woman's face lessened and she lowered the shotgun ever so slightly.

"You gotta badge?"

"Yes, yes, it's in my coat pocket." Moving slowly so as not to spook the woman Diehl retrieved his leather badge wallet and flipped it open for her.

"Bring it to me. Slowly!"

Diehl walked forward, one hand extended with the badge, the other still extended above his head.

"That's close enough." The old woman leaned forward, squinting to read the badge. Satisfied she wasn't being conned, she lowered the shotgun.

"You almost bought it, Officer – ."

"Diehl. Detective Diehl with KCPD." He quickly studied the old woman. Practical clothing, cloth apron, short-cropped hair, thin with some sort of European accent.

After fleeing the scene, Vinny crossed State Line Road and finally let off the gas, making another turn into a residential neighborhood before offering Paul additional details about the hasty getaway.

"I went around the back and up to a door with windows. I peeked inside, but it was dark. I tried the door. It was unlocked. Slowly pushed the door open and there she was. Fuckin' maid scared the shit outta me." Vinny was finally able to laugh at himself. "You'll need to check my pants, Paul."

Paul ignored Vinny's juvenile humor. He was too busy thinking of the unfruitful hours he'd spent in Kansas City after meeting Vinny in front of Union Station late the night before. Hawkins' office in a downtown Kansas City, Missouri office building was closed at mid-morning on a Monday. Locked and dark. He hadn't been seen at any of the joints where, Paul had been told, he might be found. His house was dark. Vinny almost had a hole blown through him and a nosey copper's looking for Hawkins, too.

"Let's head to Tallman's. I need to make a call. You can make some calls, too." Paul looked at Vinny. "I need to know about that copper, and what he was doing at our boy's house."

While the little woman was initially reluctant to speak to Diehl, she finally told him about the two shady characters she saw approaching the house, one heading toward the back. She grabbed Hawkins' bulky shotgun, not bothering to check if it was loaded, and hustled to the back door. She arrived just in time to meet one of the goons face-to-face, a hulking, swarthy-looking man too big for his suitcoat, opening the door to the kitchen. She described the goon's reaction as one of surprise, terror, but was greatly relieved he didn't stick around long enough to figure out she was just as scared.

She described how Hawkins had awakened her bright and early the day before. He was twitchy and clearly panicked about something. He told her he'd be out of town for a few days, pressed her to leave, too, but if she chose to stay to make the house appear empty. "Close all the drapes, turn off all the lights, and don't answer the door for anyone."

Right before he left, Hawkins told her some men might be coming to find him and it'd be best to stay clear of 'em. He then turned and hurried down the stairs with two suitcases, which he threw into the passenger seat of his Pontiac Roadster and left. She hadn't seen or heard from him since. While she wasn't sure where he'd gone, she told Diehl that Hawkins had a cabin at the remote Lake View Resort northwest of Lawrence. "It's nice," she said. "Lots of trees. A lodge. A number of cabins, and it's quite a ways out of town."

Finally, she pleaded with Diehl to find Hawkins and keep him safe. He assured her he'd do his best.

Diehl left the exclusive neighborhood and headed back toward downtown Kansas City, Kansas. Initially, he was unsure of Cap's hunch about this car theft, that there was something dodgy about it, but after the unnerving events of the past hour it was clear Cap's instincts were on target. Regardless, he thought, he needed to get back to square one. This is a car theft. Treat it like any another car theft. Find the car, arrest the thief, return the car.

Diehl turned off Minnesota onto Fourth, drove past Ann Street and parked across from the River City Bar. The smoke-filled tavern was half-full, not bad for early on a Monday evening. "Good evening, Detective Diehl," August Lenherr said flatly from behind the bar. "Business or pleasure?"

"Business, Augie," Diehl said as he reached the deserted end of the bar.

Lenherr, also bar owner and son of German immigrants, walked toward Diehl, a noticeable limp the result of a femur shattered by a German sniper round in the Meuse-Argonne Forest. Returning from France a local hero elevated the respect shown his family by many of those ignorantly inclined to assume their secret support of the Kaiser. "Whadda ya need, detective?"

"A car was stolen here Saturday night, Augie. I'm looking into it."

Augie hesitated. "Yeah, Mr. Hawkins' car."

"That's the one. You look a little surprised I know about it, Augie."

"Well, we all knew about it at the time, detective, but Mr. Hawkins made it clear to Glenda over there he didn't want the police involved." Augie glanced over his shoulder at the seductive redhead working a client twice her age. "Glenda'll tell you what you need to know."

"Thanks, Augie." Diehl said as he sidled toward the mark, flashed his badge and nodded toward the door. "Beat it, bub. Get home to the missus."

Glenda Taylor, hands on hips, watched the middle-aged businessman drain his old fashioned and shuffle away, doing her best to feign anger at losing a likely customer.

"You owe me one, Diehl."

"Yeah, yeah, yeah." Diehl said as he handed his business card to Glenda and waited for her to lose the pout. "Gabriel Hawkins had his car stolen here Saturday night. I'm investigating it. Tell me what you know, Glenda."

Diehl pulled out his notepad.

"Mr. Hawkins asked me not to tell," Glenda said, using her best eastern Kentucky drawl.

"Well, you're gonna lose that chit, Glenda." Diehl smiled. "Besides, a police report was filed."

"Well, okay." Glenda gave Diehl a rundown of the evening, including a description of the thief. "You could tell he was a rube when he walked in the door. Stuck out like a sore thumb. Pretty cocksure, too, but in a sweet kinda way, if you know what I mean. Not sure how he ended up here, but since he stole a ride, and we're close to the bus depot, we all figured he must've decided to get off the farm for an evening and came to the big city on a bus."

"How do you know he stole Mr. Hawkins' car?"

"Well, my best friend Betty Jean . . . you know Betty Jean?"

Diehl nodded.

"Well, Betty Jean told me she was earning a Lincoln out in the parking lot when she saw the rube drive off in Mr. Hawkins' car." Glenda smiled and took a sip of the drink she was nursing. "This wasn't long after he gave me his telephone number. Now how sweet is that, Detective Diehl?" Glenda smiled as she stroked the back of her fingers down Diehl's jaw.

"Just give me the number, Glenda."

## NANA'S STORY, PART TWO

Downtown Women's Hotel, first day in Los Angeles. After a brief nap in a tiny room on a surprisingly comfortable single bed, a haggard Nancy Gleason finally bathed. Hair clean, teeth clean, body clean, refreshed, Nancy headed out for food. Returning from a nearby lunch counter, she sat on the edge of her bed studying a tourist map of Hollywood. Somewhat grounded again, a plan started coming into focus. After chatting up the Widow Jenkins, Nancy hit the sidewalk with addresses on a scrap of paper and a pocketful of cash. First stop downtown was The Broadway Department Store for casual wear, fashionable, matching bling, necessities, followed by a drug store for toiletries and makeup.

Bright and early the next morning Nancy slipped into a summer dress and comfortable shoes, checked her hair and new sunglasses in the bureau mirror, grabbed her stylish parasol and headed downstairs, waving a quick goodbye to the Widow Jenkins. She hustled out into a blue-sky Los Angeles morning and walked to the terminal for a short ride on the Hollywood subway. After some navigating, Nancy successfully transferred to a blue line electric Red Car, ultimately stepping off near the swanky Beverly Hills Hotel. A short distance beyond the landmark hotel Nancy turned and wandered up Benedict Canyon Drive.

Twenty minutes into her trek, feeling a bit like she'd left the city behind after having seen only the occasional passing car, Nancy spun around at the sound of grinding gears and heavy trucks lumbering up the road from behind. Stepping back from the road she watched the trucks pass and a short distance ahead turn and disappear from sight beyond a veritable wall of hedge and trees. Picking up the pace Nancy quickly reached the private drive where the trucks turned, and without thought, followed through the estate's open gates.

Several minutes later Nancy emerged from the landscaped maturing woodland, rounded a bend of the meandering drive and caught sight again of the trucks, now lined up adjacent to a patch of perfectly manicured grass and a jaw-dropping mansion. A beehive of workers scurried about off-loading and lugging tables, chairs, a large party tent, and other accessories rented by the estate owner for a movers-and-shakers party that evening.

Nancy's attention was instantly drawn to a squat, middle-aged man clad in workman's clothes barking orders across the lawn to a group unrolling the tent's white canvas. Chin up, Nancy marched confidently to his side.

"Sir?"

The man shot a quick glance to the pretty redhead, immediately turning back toward his crew, barking more orders, this time throwing up his arms for emphasis. A stubby, mostly smoked, unlit cigar sat wedged into a corner of the barking man's lips, bouncing up and down, never once deigning an attempt at escape, the balancing act clearly born of much practice.

Satisfied the help was back on course, the man turned his attention to Nancy. "Yes, ma'am," he said, removing a sweat-stained cap and running the back of his other hand across several days of stubble.

"So, you're setting up for a wedding tonight? A party?"

The man squinted, studying Nancy before twisting around to check on his crew. Turning back, "Yeah, a big party. Huge. More liquor'n I'll drink in a lifetime." He studied Nancy again. "You got an invite?"

Nancy hesitated.

"Never mind," the man continued, "not my business. Got a big one next Saturday, too."

Nancy perked up. "Really? Where?"

The man turned and pointed beyond the lawn where his workers toiled. "Yonder across the ravine. Mr. Warner's place. Lots of guests. White tie."

"Mr. Warner?" Nancy asked.

"Jack Warner, Warner Brothers."

"Thanks, mister," Nancy said as she pivoted, twirling her parasol as she hustled down the drive.

The next morning following breakfast Nancy returned to The Broadway for sandals, shorts, a stylish blouse, sleepwear, undies and new luggage. That evening after bathing, a resolute Nancy Gleason packed her new luggage, tossing all that was Nancy Gleason to a corner of the room, save for the bundles of cash. Foxy Storm was no longer the implausible fantasy of a desperately lonely girl sitting for hours in front of a small, cracked mirror in a cramped bedroom. Foxy Storm was born, and there was no looking back.

The following morning a taxi turned off Sunset Boulevard and onto the drive leading up to the Beverly Hills Hotel, offloading the smartly dressed Foxy Storm. A short time later Foxy followed her luggage and a young bellhop into a room overlooking the palm tree-lined hotel drive. "Oh my goodness," Foxy murmured to herself as she took stock of the room. She'd only seen such elegance in the movies. Fresh flowers in a cut crystal vase, fine cotton sheets on a full-size bed, and her very own bathroom.

Everything was perfect. Foxy threw out her arms and fell backward onto the bed, lying motionless as she stared at the ceiling, savoring the moment. After a few moments the bathtub called.

Later, luggage unpacked, Foxy returned to the hotel's lobby, striding across the gleaming tile floor to the front desk with important questions. A few moments after being politely asked to sit and wait, a kindly, aging man emerged and approached Foxy.

He smiled. "May I join you? I'm told you registered earlier. Here for the week?"

Foxy nodded.

The man settled into a cushioned club chair. "How can I help you, Miss, uh . . ."

"Storm. Foxy Storm. My father's a rich cattle baron from the Flint Hills. He sent me out here to pursue my dream of being an actress."

The man rubbed his chin. "Hmm, well, okay. Where are the Flint Hills?"

"Kansas."

"And you're here to become an actress?"

"Yessir."

"Okay, well, how may I help you?"

Foxy leaned in, lowering her voice. "I've got two questions. No, three questions. First, who do I tip, and how much?"

The man nodded.

"My second question is where can I get something to eat?"

The man smiled. "Easy enough. And your third question?"

Foxy cleared her throat. "How can I get an invitation to Jack Warner's party on Saturday night?"

The man smiled, tilting his head. "Not so easy. They're not movie tickets, you know."

"So, I can't swing it? I can't go to the party?"

The man leaned back, crossing his legs. "If you don't mind, how old are you?"

"Twenty-four."

The man smiled.

"Twenty-two?" Foxy offered.

Still smiling, the man fished an engraved case from his breast pocket and removed a cigarette.

"Okay, I'm nineteen years old," Foxy finally admitted.

The man leaned forward. "Ms. Storm, join me in the lounge. You can eat, I'll have a smoke. We'll talk tips and see what we can come up with regarding Mr. Warner's party."

No sooner had the two had settled into chairs at a table in a corner of hotel lounge than a waiter was there to take their order. "A club sandwich and lemonade for our guest, William, and scones and tea for me, please."

"Yes sir."

After the waiter departed, the man gave Foxy a quick tutorial on tipping. "Moving on then, why the interest in Mr. Warner's party. Mr. Lloyd had one Saturday night. A week from now someone else will be having a party."

"Warner Brothers, sir. They make movies. They make movie stars."

"And you think…"

"Yes, I do." Foxy said seriously. "I can act. I've practiced my whole life. And I'm pretty."

The man smiled as he tapped ash from his cigarette.

"Well, I'm pretty enough," Foxy said with a hint of defiance.

The man laughed. "No, no, no, I'm sorry, you're very pretty. I was just thinking of your moxie."

"My what?"

"Your moxie, er, your nerve, your fearlessness."

"Oh. Thank you, I think."

The man rubbed out his cigarette as their orders arrived. "And you can act?" he asked after the waiter had turned and left.

Foxy nodded. "Been practicing my whole life," she said with a mouth full of sandwich.

The man smiled.

Foxy swallowed and washed it down with a gulp of lemonade. "You seem to smile a lot. I'm thinkin' you find me amusing."

The man considered the observation. "Well, it's a little more nuanced than that. See, at my age I've done most everything, seen most everything, but then this incredibly unique, breath of fresh air falls into my lap." He laughed. "Excuse me for mixing metaphors."

"Pardon me?"

"I'll help you. No promises, and at best maybe we get you past the front door. How long you stay is another thing altogether."

Foxy beamed. "You'll help me? Yes?"

"Yes."

"Oh, you're the sweetest man ever," Foxy gushed.

"No, but thank you." The man signaled to the waiter. "A Bordeaux and one glass, William." He turned his attention back to Foxy. "Okay, first thing you do is lose the chewing gum, the gum you were chomping on when we first met."

Foxy stopped mid-bite, looking up at the man.

He smiled. "You can chew again after you've become famous."

The man pulled out a pocket notepad and pen, and over the next hour several pages were filled with thoughts, names, stores, clothing, jewelry.

"Hold on, Nana," Megan said, holding up a hand. "I need to change cassettes."

"Thoughts so far?"

"Well, clearly, it's all new." Megan paused. "I'm anxious to hear about the Warner party, how that turned out."

"It's comin', Kiddo."

Megan pushed the record button. "Okay, Nana, tell me about the party you crashed."

Shadows covered the drive as the shiny limo eased to a stop under the Beverly Hills Hotel tile-roof portico. The driver slid out from behind the wheel, gave his jacket a quick tug, adjusted his cap and hustled around the car, opening the rear door with a smile for the stunning redhead. Foxy's unadorned white satin evening gown clung tightly at the hips, accented by tasteful diamond earrings, a simple diamond necklace, and a small red handbag.

It was a short drive to the Warner estate off Angelo Drive. Since she had chosen to arrive fashionably late, Foxy's limo waited in line, inching forward on the estate drive until finally circling a fountain and reaching the front door of the movie mogul's Spanish-style mansion. As the limo stopped, a white-tie attired, hulking young man stepped forward, opened Foxy's car door and offered his hand. Foxy swung her legs out and stood, flashing a confident smile to the young man while quickly scanning the mansion entrance. She noted two more white-tie attired young men stationed on either side of the open doorway. Live music mixed with a jumble of voices and bursts of laughter spilled out onto the drive.

Foxy stepped to the side as the young greeter met the next car, offloading a dusty Studebaker full of boisterous, already tipsy young people. As this group collected and marched toward the front door Foxy slipped in at their rear, nodding and smiling along with the partiers as they passed the centurions. Safely inside, Foxy slipped away from the group, exiting the entryway into a huge room alive with Hollywood's elite, a small band cranking it out from the far end.

Alone and suddenly uncertain, Foxy grabbed a drink off the tray of a passing server and sought safe harbor with an older couple standing silently nearby at the party's edge. Steeling herself, Foxy thrust herself into the surprised couple's space, smiling, talking non-stop. Before the couple had a chance to engage the hyper stranger, Foxy excused herself and weaved through the crowded room, landing with a small knot of know-it-all businessman types before drifting on to another older couple.

Two drinks down and feeling confident she was there for the evening, Foxy's eyes darted between laughter and small talk, surveying the room for the mustachioed party host. Reaching for a passing drink Foxy was oblivious to the Warner bouncer who stole up behind her. She froze as a massive hand placed a vise-grip on one bare shoulder, and a raspy voice whispered in her ear, "No scene, we're leaving."

The man turned Foxy slowly. A chiseled face smiled wryly down at her, but then his eyes shot up, looking beyond Foxy. The goon's smug look immediately turned sheepish, respectful as he dropped the grip and stepped back, mumbling something apologetic to the presence behind Foxy before wheeling about and disappearing among the guests.

Foxy knew there was someone standing behind her. Before turning to shower praise on the white knight who'd come to her rescue, she imagined it was someone influential, powerful enough to wobble a bodyguard's knees. In that fleeting moment she imagined Jack Warner himself saying something soothing, apologizing profusely for the buffoonery of his man, and inviting Foxy Storm into his universe.

Smiling, Foxy turned to face her savior. Her smile immediately morphed into one of quizzical bemusement as she stared into the kind face of an olive-skinned man as imposing as the one he'd scared away, but twice the young man's age.

Foxy tapped the last Camel from the soft pack, holding the empty pack aloft until catching Gonzalo's attention.

"Nana! You can't stop now. So, you're not kicked out of the party?"

"Button, this is where I met Big Jimmy."

"Oh my goodness, Nana."

Megan listened as Foxy described the beginning of a love story, her love for a man of few words and a calm voice. Mature, with a big heart.

"Big Jimmy was just standing there when the goon turned me around. He didn't say a word, but the goon let loose of me and disappeared. Big Jimmy offered his arm. I slid mine through his. Reflexively, like I was hypnotized. He led me outside to a table on the patio." Foxy smiled wistfully. "We talked for hours.

"Did he tell you he was in the Mafia, Nana?"

Foxy smiled. "No, he gave me his card. All it said was his name, and the word 'Businessman.'"

"So, what drew him to you? Why was he 'just standing there?'"

"Well, Big Jimmy was with Mr. Warner when I snuck in, then started acting like I owned the place, like I knew everyone." Foxy laughed. "You get that kind of swagger growin' up in a small town. I don't think it ever goes away. Maybe it gets muted a bit once you discover there's a whole big world out there." Foxy lit the Camel and took a big drag.

"And Big Jimmy was drawn to you . . ."

"Umm, yes, I'm flitting around being a chatter-mouth and here's Big Jimmy and Mr. Warner watching me prance around. They were amused. I was their entertainment. Finally, Mr. Warner announces 'enough's enough, time for her to go.' Tells his goon not to make a scene. But Big Jimmy, he's already got a crush on me. He's a widower. No kids. Lost his wife a couple years earlier. He follows the goon and the rest is history."

"Ahh, Nana, and just like that, you found your soulmate."

Two days later Foxy moved out of the Beverly Hills Hotel and into Big Jimmy's Bel Air home. Two months later they were married. Nine months after the party, Little Jimmy was born.

"Dearie, less than two weeks after that party I was at the Warner Brothers lot, on a set, in costume, shooting my only scene in a very forgettable western. Turns out I stole my first scene." Foxy laughed. "My only line in the movie was 'hold on there.' Well, I thought I could do better. So, what I said with the camera rolling was 'hold your horses there, cowboy.'" Foxy growled, reliving the moment. "'Cut, cut, cut,' the director screamed. That drew a few laughs from the crew. Well, he made me do it again, using the line in the script, but when the movie came out it had my line." Foxy smiled triumphantly, taking another drag. "And it got noticed. People liked it. They liked me. So, they gave me better roles, more lines, more scenes, until I'm gettin' my name on the marquee."

"That's a great story, Nana."

Foxy continued. "I thought maybe I'd messed everything up before I really got going. A couple years later. Errol Flynn, another Jack Warner party. Flynn was – "

Excited, Megan interrupted. "Yes, yes, you punched him out. Knocked him into the pool. A story in The Hollywood Reporter."

Foxy shook her head slowly. "What actually happened is Flynn was drunk and a little handsy with me. He was always drunk, always a little handsy with the ladies." Foxy took a sip. "But he went a little far and I slapped him. He grabbed my arm and jerked me around. Bogie, Humphrey Bogart, he's standing right there, and he jumps between us, and quick as a whip he punches Flynn in the chest."

"The chest? He punched him in the chest?"

"Cupcake, back in those days movies were like cars on an assembly line. We're churnin' 'em out one after another. Everyone's workin' on something. A black eye, broken nose, means production stops, money lost." Foxy smiled. "So, yes, Bogie hit him straight in the chest. Knocked him into the pool. It all played better if the scrappy Foxy Storm did the deed."

"Interesting. So you didn't get in trouble?"

"Thought I would, but nope, my star was rising. Couple days later, Big Jimmy visits Flynn's set. Hangs back for an hour. Doesn't speak to Flynn, but Flynn got the message loud and clear."

"It was all meant to be, Nana." Megan said as she rifled through her notepad, mentioning press references to Big Jimmy's ties to La Cosa Nostra. The tax evasion conviction that sent him to prison in the early 1960s, from which he received an early parole due to terminal cancer. The unnamed FBI source describing Big Jimmy's role as liaison between the mob and Hollywood.

"Well, this might add a little color to Big Jimmy," Foxy added. "Big Jimmy refused to have anything to do with Vegas."

Megan looked stumped.

"Las Vegas wasn't always Las Vegas. Before that nutjob Siegel got hold of it, Vegas was just a sleepy little desert town. It was Bugsy Siegel, an L.A. mobster, who turned it into a gambling mecca."

"Big Jimmy didn't think it would work?"

"Just the opposite, Sweetie. He knew it would work. He could see it. Dollars, dollars, more dollars, and dead bodies from mobsters fightin' over the money." Foxy rubbed out her cigarette and took a drink. "He stayed a million miles away from Las Vegas."

Death came swift for Big Jimmy following his mercy parole. Within six months Foxy was hosting his wake in the couple's comfortable Bel Air home, filled with Tinseltown's elite and all manner of large men talking with Jersey accents, there to pay respect.

The next six months were spent unearthing previously unknown wealth squirreled away over the decades. Big Jimmy was, indeed, a good businessman, and something of a money packrat. Large tracts of land, numerous safe deposit boxes spread across town, each stuffed with cash, bundles of cash in random nooks and crannies of the house, car trunk, tool shed, pool house. Almost every day was a new discovery.

Save for a one-day cameo in yet another dime-a-dozen, low budget California beach movie shot at Malibu with a fresh-faced crop of stardom hopefuls wearing next to nothing, following Big Jimmy's death Foxy withdrew from everything remotely Hollywood. Though she'd not acted in more than a decade, before Big Jimmy's passing she'd regularly appeared at galas, award ceremonies. She'd stayed connected with the industry. Grounded. Everything changed when Big Jimmy died.

At the persistent urging of Foxy's concerned, long-time attorney, a well-meaning dear friend, Foxy finally sought help from the attorney's personal psychologist, a gentle young woman who cracked the code, launching Foxy toward the next phase of her life, a passionate crusade in support of endangered animals. It gave Foxy purpose and, in hindsight, seemed so obvious to the former actress who'd never met a mangy dog she didn't want to adopt.

# WEST BOTTOMS

# TUESDAY, JULY 10, 1934, MORNING

"Diehl!" Diehl looked across the squad room and saw Captain Mulroney standing in his office doorway. "Join me. Now."

Diehl returned to his trusty Underwood and quickly pecked a few more keys. Satisfied the detailed report was finished, he pulled it from the typewriter and hustled over to the captain's office.

"Shut the door and close the shades, Diehl, then grab a seat," Mulroney said, removing an unlit cigar from his mouth as Diehl eased into a chair across the desk. "I've checked the Missouri plate you gave me." Mulroney fished around on his cluttered desk and retrieved a scrap of paper. "That Ford you saw last night is registered to Northland Salvage." He looked at Diehl. "Know anything about Northland Salvage?"

"Heard of it, I think, but that's it."

"Well," Mulroney continued, "it's a front for Tommy Lozarro. The Lozarro mob. Pretty much an all-cash business. Any idea why they're messin' around with this?"

"Nope," Diehl shook his head, "but it fits with what little I've learned." He handed the report across to the captain. "Your eyes only, right?"

"Yup, it all stays inside this room, Diehl." Mulroney returned the unlit cigar to his mouth. "The phone number you gave me to check is for a house in Flint, Kansas. It's a one-dog town a little southwest of Topeka." He unfolded a map and the two leaned forward.

"Here it is Diehl. Head out of Topeka on 40 and then it's maybe ten, twelve miles straight south on Flint Road. Here's the address."

"Pretty good chance the car's there, Cap, or someone there's seen it." Diehl stood to leave. "It's where I'm headed."

Diehl took a step toward the door, stopped and turned back. "Oh yeah, the woman at Hawkins' house said he owns a cabin at Lake View Resort outside of Lawrence. Maybe he's hiding out there. Dunno, but I'll check it out on my way back from Flint. I've got some questions for him."

Mulroney nodded. "Watch your back, Diehl. You've upped the ante."

Diehl nodded and opened the office door, crashing into Detective Brandt as he stepped out, upending a cup of coffee down Brandt's unpressed white shirt. "Jesus, Diehl, watch where you're going. Fuck."

"Here to see Cap?" Diehl asked the flustered Brandt.

"Fuck yourself, pretty boy."

Diehl bit his tongue as Brandt turned and wandered back across the squad room to his desk, dabbing his soaked shirt with a handkerchief pulled from a pants pocket.

Paul's suite at The Aladdin in downtown Kansas City, Missouri was a short four blocks from Tallman's Grill, a ten-minute walk for the fit mobster. Vinny waited outside Tallman's, flicking away a half-smoked Lucky Strike as Paul approached. "I got a table for us in the back, Paul," Vinny said, opening the door for the younger man.

The two walked through the grill's lunch-time crowd and into the kitchen. "There's an office behind the kitchen, Paul. Want somethin' to eat?"

Paul shook his head. "I'm good, Vinny."

Vinny shouted across the kitchen. "Hey, Tony, a plate of Pasta alla Norma. Some extra ricotta, too. And some bread."

Paul followed Vinny into a cramped office and shut the door behind them. "Whadda ya got, Vinny?"

"Well, you were right. The guy we saw at your boy's house last night is a Kansas copper. Diehl. Last name's Diehl. Played basketball for Phog Allen over in Lawrence. A college boy, rising star in their department."

"What's he doing there, Vinny?"

"Here's where it gets a little weird, Paul. Hawkins' daddy has some pull, so they've got their top guy investigating a car theft. Your boy's car was stolen."

"Hawkins' dad is involved, Vinny?" Paul asked.

"I dunno, but the dad's a big enough deal they've got this Diehl guy trying to track down the car. We've done some shit with the dad, too, if you know what I mean."

Vinny continued. "So, it's all hush-hush there at Metro. Just Diehl and his boss."

Paul propped a foot on the small desk and leaned back against the wall, staring at the high ceiling. "We need to find the car, Vinny," Paul said matter-of-factly after a moment. "Our package is in the car. Where's the car, Vinny?"

"Flint, Kansas," Vinny said. "Well, maybe in Flint, Kansas. The perp's from Flint."

"Any idea where we can find Hawkins? The boy."

"Oh yeah," Vinny perked up. "He might be hidin' out at a lake near Lawrence. He's gotta cabin there."

"Know where it's at, Vinny?"

"Oh yeah," Vinny smiled, "Been there for a wedding. I know exactly where it's at."

"Okay, we stop there first. Let's gas up and go."

Diehl slowed the Studebaker as he crested a rise, the sleepy, tiny Kansas town of Flint laid out before him. The hamlet was an oasis of elm and oak trees in a sea of gently rolling hills sprinkled with fields of heat-stressed corn and shade-seeking cattle. On the far side of the town of several hundred souls, near the road that climbed out of the narrow river valley, a spindly metal water tower tank displayed the town's name.

The dusty, crushed limestone road he'd traveled since turning off the modern, concrete highway thirty minutes earlier ended at a rickety two-lane steel bridge over the lazy, muddy Wakarusa River, now little bigger than a creek in the middle of a bone-dry Midwest summer, but capable of raging, violent destruction.

Crossing the bridge, Diehl cruised forward the length of Flint's two-block business district. The only sign of life at mid-afternoon were two old-timers in overalls and straw hats sharing a bench in the shade of the five-and-dime sidewalk awning. Diehl nodded at the old timers and scanned the mostly deserted business district. At the end of the brick main street he pulled up and parked in the front of the city hall, which also served as home to the one-man police force.

Having jettisoned his suit coat and tie, the parched Diehl brushed limestone dust from his dark pants before walking into city hall. A matronly woman behind the counter eyed him. "Can I help you, mister?"

"Yes, ma'am, I'd like to speak to the police chief. Please."

"Chief Mooney 'specting you?"

"Yes, ma'am. We spoke by telephone late this morning."

A loud voice came from the back. "Detective Diehl?"

Diehl looked down a hallway behind the clerk to see a burly man sporting a shiny star on the chest of his khaki, long-sleeved shirt, emerge from an office near the back of the building. "C'mon back, detective."

Diehl thanked the clerk and walked around the countern and down the hallway taking notice of numerous framed photos of the town's treeless early days.

Diehl shut the door behind him and joined Chief Mooney in his small office. "So," the Chief began, "you're lookin' for a stolen green Ford. That correct?"

"Yessir. A '31 green Ford convertible. Technically, balsam green." Diehl paused, smiling. "Actually, balsam green is just a fancy way of saying 'green mixed with gray.' Kind of a gray-green color. Like a dusty green."

The chief threw back his head and let out a belly laugh. "Damn, son, I drove all around town after we talked this morning, looking for a green Ford rag top. I'm thinkin' green, like tree leaves." He smiled. "Course, you can drive this town in about ten minutes."

The chief continued. "The address for that telephone number, 231 Lincoln, it's a rental. Car's not there. No car's there right now. Renter is Jimmy Cooper, a young guy from here in town. A few years outta high school, I'm pretty sure." The Chief nodded his head toward the middle of town. "Dad and granddaddy own the bank back there on the corner, but Jimmy's a little rough 'round the edges, if you know what I mean. Not exactly the banker type. Busts his knuckles at the lumber yard 'cross the way."

Diehl rose from his seat. "Let's go see him."

The Chief motioned Diehl back down to his chair. "I took the liberty to stop by and talk to Mel, the lumberyard owner. Jimmy's not there today. Mel said that's not unusual. Went back by his house and talked to a couple of neighbors. They've no idea where he's at."

Diehl stood, "Well, Chief, I need to make a stop over by Lawrence before it gets dark. Here's my card. You know the car we're looking for. And we've got cause to hold this Cooper guy." Diehl looked back from the doorway. "Give me a call when you grab him."

Development of the snobby Lake View Resort started in 1919. The remote location was tucked away in an area of age-old cottonwoods a few miles mostly west of Lawrence and adjacent to a former loop of the Kansas River. At some point in the distant past the river flooded, cutting a new channel in the area and bypassing the former channel when the flood waters receded. It left behind what's commonly referred to as an "elbow lake," the shape of the former river channel.

The resort included a rustic, rough-hewn wood lodge with covered seating areas along the front and sides, high ceilings with electric fans, screened windows along each wall, a large open room with a small stage and giant stone fireplace at the room's far end, and a bar and dining area near the front of the building. The property manager's office was off the bar and dining area, near the front door.

The resort included thirty or so small cabins, rustic in appearance but including electricity, running water, gas, plumbing and telephones, located on several randomly winding and looping gravel roads through the ancient forest. Most were leased on a long-term basis and used sporadically, with several set aside for short-term rental. There were no permanent residents at the resort. A road and several foot paths led to the lake, small marina and swimming area.

Paul stepped out of the lodge and returned to the car where Vinny waited, smoking a cigarette. "The manager said Hawkins' cabin is close to the lake." Paul said. "Take this road to the first left, then follow it to a fork. Go left at the fork. It's the second cabin on the right after the fork. He was there an hour ago when they ran some lunch over to him."

Paul and Vinny followed the directions and within no time were approaching Hawkins' cabin, his Pontiac Roadster just off the narrow road in front of the cabin.

"Drive on by, Vinny."

After following a loop in the drive, Paul signaled Vinny to pull over. "I'm gonna grab somethin' from the trunk. I'll cut over and cover the back. Gimme a couple minutes, then pull up and park behind his car. Go up and see if he'll answer the door."

Paul grabbed a canvas tote from the trunk, then returned to the passenger window. "Vinny, remember, we need some information from him."

With that reminder, the young mobster was off through the shadowy forest underbrush.

# TUESDAY, JULY 10, 1934, LATE AFTERNOON

Cottonwood leaves glimmered in the late afternoon sun as Diehl pulled up in front of the Lake View Resort lodge. It had been a sweaty, dusty day for the Kansas City detective. He trudged up the steps to the covered front porch and walked through the open front door into the dining area. Not a soul was in sight. Hearing a noise off to the side of the small bar he wandered over to an open door.

"Hello. You in charge here?"

"Damn," the manager yelped as he swiveled around in his chair, clearly spooked by Diehl's appearance. "Damn, I'm sorry. Just filing away some invoices. Didn't hear ya come in."

Diehl flashed his badge for the slightly built, balding man. "Detective Diehl, Kansas City PD. Just need some information on one of your guests."

The manager stood and leaned forward, glancing at the badge and back at Diehl. Convinced he was speaking to the law the manager nodded. "Sure. How can we help?"

"You gotta man named Hawkins staying here? Gabriel Hawkins."

"Well, Mr. Hawkins is a popular man, that's fer sure," the manager said. "Yeah, he's here. His cabin's down near the lake."

"A popular man?"

"Yeah, detective, he had some business associates here to see him maybe an hour ago."

Diehl reached into his breast pocket and pulled out his notepad. "Two men? Well dressed? Driving a Ford with Missouri plates?"

The manager paused briefly before answering. "Yes, yes, yes, and I don't know. Didn't notice the plates. Only met one of 'em, but watched as the two of 'em drove off. Said they were here to get some contracts signed. Pronto. Time is money. Needed to see Mr. Hawkins as soon as possible."

"Take me there, mister, uh - "

"Lewis. Sam Lewis."

Diehl scribbled down the manager's name and returned the notepad to his breast pocket. "You can ride with me."

Vinny drove slowly along the river road just west of Lawrence, each man scanning the tree lines and challenged crop fields for movement. "We ain't gonna find him, Paul. He's hoofing it somewhere."

"He must've seen us drive by, Vinny. Guy's pretty scared to take off through the woods like that," Paul pointed east toward Kansas City. "Let's head back to town. I need a bath. You can make a call."

Diehl and Lewis pulled to the side of the lane and parked behind Hawkins' roadster. Diehl stopped Lewis from opening his car door. "Hang on a second, Mr. Lewis. You stay here."

Diehl lifted out his revolver and checked the cylinder. "I'll let you know if I need you."

Diehl got out, careful not to slam the car door behind him. He crept slowly along the driver's side of Hawkins' roadster, the revolver cupped in both hands. The seats were empty. The engine hood was slightly open, so he pulled it up and looked into the engine compartment. The engine wiring looked like spaghetti. Someone – likely Hawkins' visitors, Diehl figured – had disabled the car.

Diehl quietly approached the cabin front door, eyes peeled for any sign of

BRAZIER & THORNTON

movement. Resting his shoulder against the door jamb Diehl reached over to the door handle and turned it slowly. Diehl kicked it open with the side of his foot and leapt in, crouching as he swung from side to side, his revolver in both hands at arms' length. The small living room and equally small dining room were empty. He inched down the short hallway and peered into the bedroom, then the bathroom. Both were empty. Also empty was the functional kitchen at the back of the cabin. The back door was ajar.

Satisfied the cabin was empty, Diehl retraced his steps to the front to survey the carnage. Framed pictures were torn apart and laying on the polished wood floor. Divan and chair pillows were slashed and torn apart. Furniture was upended. Drawers were ripped out of the small wood desk in the corner of the room, contents strewn about the floor. The room was a total mess. Same for each of the other rooms. The cabin had been turned upside down by someone looking for something.

Diehl did a mental summary and arrived at a conclusion: whoever was looking for Hawkins didn't find him. No blood spatters. The car was disabled. The cabin had been searched from top to bottom, an act likely not necessary if the bad guy, or bad guys, had hold of Hawkins.

Diehl stepped out onto the front porch and waved at Lewis to join him. He led the manager into the cabin and, after the horrified manager surveyed damage, gave him some direction. "Here's my card. I gotta get back to Kansas City. Call your sheriff and get him out here to do a report," Diehl instructed. "Tell him what you told me, show him the car engine, and call me if anything else comes up. Anything."

An hour later Diehl pulled into the mostly empty police parking lot at HQ. He was sweaty and hungry, and ready to be done for the day, but was anxious to see if Flint's Chief Mooney had called with news. The squad room was deserted, most of the detectives likely being home for the evening or out grabbing a bite to eat. As he reached his desk, he saw Detective Brandt walk out of Captain Mulroney's dark office.

"Hey, Brandt," Diehl shouted across the room, "Cap in there?"

Brandt stopped short, surprised to see Diehl. "No Diehl, he's gone for the night." Brandt turned his back and started to walk away, but stopped and turned toward Diehl. "Oh yeah, a Chief Mooney called for ya maybe twenty

85

minutes ago. No sign yet of the stolen Ford, but he's hot on it for ya."

"What're you doing answering my phone, Brandt?"

"Just trying to help, Diehl. G'night." And with that Brandt was gone, his plodding, heavy steps on the old wooden stairs echoing through the quiet squad room.

Paul threw on the hotel's Turkish cotton robe and walked out into his suite to answer the telephone. The operator connected him to Vinny. "We've got pasta and meatballs over here at Tallman's, and I've got some more information. Want me to pick ya up?"

"Thirty minutes, downstairs."

Exactly thirty minutes later Vinny pulled up in front of The Aladdin. Paul opened the passenger side door and got in, and the two rode in silence the short distance to Tallman's. After weaving through the packed club's evening crowd Vinny and Paul sat down at a small table at the end of the narrow, bustling kitchen. Empty wine glasses, silverware, cloth napkins and an opened bottle of red wine took up most of the table top. No sooner had they sat down but one of the kitchen help brought plates heaped with pasta and large meatballs, and a loaf of bread. Vinny filled both glasses with wine, stuck an end of the napkin inside his collar, and ripped off the end of the bread loaf.

"You said you've got some news, Vinny?"

Vinny held up a finger and gulped some wine to help him chew his mouth full of bread. After wiping his mouth he leaned forward to keep from speaking too loudly. "Okay, my guy tells me your boy was in a Kansas bar when his car was stolen. The River View. Just across the river. His car's a green Ford rag-top. Pretty new. There's a hooker who works the bar. Linda? Glenda? No, Glenda. Redhead. She might know somethin'."

"Finish up, Vinny. We got work to do."

## NANA'S STORY, PART THREE

"So, umm, Nana, can we back up to Nancy Gleason, Kansas, and, uh, the stolen car, the suitcase full of cash?"

"Yes, but not without my other Jimmy. My first Jimmy. My first time being in love."

"Nana! Okay, okay, hold on, let me check the tape. Order another drink or more cigarettes, or whatever. I gotta get this."

A moment later, ready for more, Megan nodded.

"So, Sweetie, my first Jimmy, my first time being in love. We were just kids, really. Let me give you the lead up to Jimmy Dale. That okay?"

"Of course."

Foxy gave a bit more detail of her lonely childhood in a cloistered, tiny Kansas town. Pickford Falls. The additional detail didn't include the time the awkward fourteen-year-old slipped out of the school's bandbox gymnasium with a senior class boy during a Friday night high school basketball game, anxious for her first kiss, her first love, only to end up fighting off one hand up her homemade dress while the other fumbled to fit between buttons of her hand-me-down blouse.

Blouse ripped, hair disheveled, crying uncontrollably, the newly initiated teen ran two blocks to the arms of her consoling mother.

Foxy also didn't reveal the following Monday morning every student and likely all of the teachers in the small school, in the small town of Pickford Falls, where everyone knew everyone else, had heard the senior boy's version of Friday night, or an enhanced, second-hand version of it. Now they all knew the poor little redhead wasn't just a poor little redhead from across the tracks, but she was the white trash little redhead. Easy. Loose. Prob'ly got it from her mother.

No, Megan didn't learn everything. Best that some of the past remain buried.

"My first kiss wasn't that remarkable, Muffin."

As much as anything, what made life worth living for Nancy Gleason, the town tramp who'd never reached second base with a boy, were the summers she spent in nearby Topeka, the big city, with her outgoing cousin Anna Mae and Aunt Ruth, her momma's big sister. The girls were the same age and inseparable.

Aunt Ruth worked in the State Capitol building doing something with record-keeping. Whatever it was, there was always enough money for matinee movies, trolley rides out to Gage Park and its enormous pool, and the occasional picnic. And, despite Aunt Ruth's stern warnings to keep their distance from the boys, the girls, invariably led by the precocious Anna Mae, spent much of their pool time flirting with the boys.

The idyllic summers for young Nancy Gleason came to an abrupt end before her high school senior year when Anna Mae, maybe two months pregnant, was shipped off to Falls City, Nebraska to live with momma and Aunt Ruth's younger sister.

The cousins stayed in touch, chiefly through cards and letters, though nothing could replace the rare telephone calls. Several months after the birth of her baby girl Anna Mae took a job at the Missouri Pacific depot on the south edge of town, daily updating the succeeding seven day's expected arrivals.

Back in Pickford Falls, meanwhile, though the maturing redhead clutched tightly to her dream of stardom, of late she'd become infatuated with the exploits of Bonnie Parker and Clyde Barrow, and heartthrob Charles "Pretty Boy" Floyd. She devoured every word of every sensationalized story reported in otherwise unread newspapers stacked up in her school's library. The cracked mirror in her spartan bedroom, before which she'd mastered every emotion, every facial expression she'd need to become a Hollywood star, now doubled for Bonnie Parker scowls and threatening demands to "Stick 'em up!" Nancy begged her mother for a beret like Bonnie wore. Store-bought or hand-made, it didn't matter.

Daydreaming about being on the lam, robbing banks and fleeing the hapless police only grew following high school. The daydreams were fueled by the almost unbearable tedium of a dead-end job at the local grain elevator, where Nancy pretended to laugh at men's stupid jokes, feigned interest at their haughty opinions on the economy or politics, and expertly deflected the never-ending innuendoes, leers, unwelcome strokes and hugs by men, married men twice her age and older, and especially from Merrill Johnson, the grain elevator manager, her boss. All the while she took care not to cross the invisible but very real line over which she'd most certainly lose her job, at a time when jobs were mighty hard to find.

Nancy Gleason was no longer the awkward girl, but now a young woman. At night, alone, she'd stare in the mirror, thinking maybe she was actually pretty, but insecure enough not to wholly believe it. She'd lay awake in the only bed she'd ever known, concocting schemes that might lift her from her God-forsaken town, from Kansas. Often, she fantasized about a life of crime, the thrill she imagined of staring down a meek bank teller, making off with a sack of cash, the heroine she'd be to the downtrodden homeless when she handed out part of the loot.

Nancy Gleason's inflection point was recognizing if she wanted to break away, wanted to pursue her dreams, she'd need money, lots of money. Crime was the only way, she concluded.

But how? Critically, how to do it and not get caught? Finally, after countless nights of scheming herself to sleep, the perfect plan came like a vision special delivery from God himself. An epiphany. And even a nineteen-year-old nobody could pull it off. She'd break in to the grain elevator late at night, plant incriminating evidence pointing to the boozer Merrill Johnson, and make off with a safe full of grain receipts. Now, she simply needed to stitch the plan together, check and re-check.

"It'd all come together in my head by the time I met Jimmy Dale Cooper."

"Is he still alive, Nana?"

"No, no, Kiddo. He's gone, like everyone else. But that boy was a dust devil. Born charismatic."

*Early July, 1934.* Head down, hustling toward the grain elevator office door, Nancy Gleason was cornered by the yard hand, Joe, a young guy from Flint she generally tried to avoid, asking if she'd like to meet up with his buddy Jimmy for a blind date the next night. Over in Flint. At the bowling alley.

"Oh yeah, his daddy owns the bank," Joe added with a wink.

Nancy hesitated. "So, he's a banker?"

Joe doubled over laughing. "Jimmy, a banker? Far from it. He'll never be a banker. He's more likely to be a bank robber." He laughed even harder.

"Oh, really. Yeah, sure, I'll meet him."

Jimmy Dale Cooper, only child of the local banker, grandson of the bank owner, was something of a big fish in the small pond of Flint, Kansas, a bigger small town upstream of Pickford Falls, and a couple years older than the future movie star.

As a young teen, Jimmy was permanently banned from the local general store for repeated shoplifting. He was unceremoniously booted from the University of Kansas his freshman year for stealing and pawning a fraternity brother's golf clubs, and shortly after returning home Jimmy Dale's disgusted grandfather forever barred him from the bank for stealing from the cash drawer.

The bans, the disgust, the anger directed at him only fueled Jimmy's rebelliousness. When alone with his loyal circle of Jimmy Dale worshippers the small-town banking family heir boldly claimed disinterest with anything remotely resembling a respectable career, though trading on the family name quickly landed him a job at the lumberyard.

Megan held up her hand. "Okay, let's back up. This Jimmy's your first true love?"

"Yes."

"You're nineteen and he's, uh, maybe twenty-one?"

"Yes."

"You meet him at a bowling alley on a blind date?"

"Yes."

"In the meantime, you've cooked up a way to steal money from where you work and make it look like your boss did it?"

"Yes, we pulled off the heist two days later. The cops arrested Merrill Johnson, my boss. We got more than $5,300. Everyone thought he was siphoning off cash."

"Okay, 'we?'"

"Me and Jimmy."

"The boy you just met? The banker's son? And you did this for only $5,000?"

"Well, that was a lot of money in 1934. You could buy a small house with that kind of money."

"Nana, you realize how crazy this all sounds, right? And what's a 'dust devil?'"

Foxy laughed. "A dust devil's like a little rope tornado that springs up outta nowhere when it's hot and dry, spinning like crazy for a few seconds, then disappearing quick as it came. You're lucky to see one. Maybe it's just a Midwest thing. Doubt you've ever seen one in Connecticut. Jimmy, Jimmy Dale, was like that. He burned white hot and flamed out quickly."

"Hmm, you know this all sounds pretty bonkers?"

Foxy smiled, pondering the question. "Well, saying it out loud does make it sound a little crazy." She lit another Camel and leaned back. "But it's my story, and I haven't even told you about the stolen car, the gangsters, the train station heist and the G-men."

Laughing, Megan tossed her notepad on the table. "There's more?"

"Yes, yes, much more. Not what you expected, I'll bet?"

"No, Nana, not at all. But I'm lovin' it."

"Well, it all fits together."

Foxy described her blind date with Jimmy. "After a couple beers he's talkin' a mile a minute. He's talkin' stealin' this, stealin' that. The boy's family owns the bank and he's sweatin' at the lumberyard. I was hypnotized. Everyone he sees he's tellin' 'em to 'keep it on the sunny side.'"

"What? He's telling people what?"

Foxy smiled. "It was his catchphrase, Cupcake, though after a few days it was kinda driving me nuts."

"Hmm, boys are different, Nana."

"Yup, they are, Sweetie. At any rate, I take a chance and tell Jimmy about my plan. My goodness, girl, it was like the boy won the lottery. He's throwin' out ideas left and right. His brain flipped into high gear. No way that boy ever works at a bank."

"So, Nana, how's the rest of the story fit together? You, the G-men, the train heist?"

"Train station, Sweetie. We robbed a train station, not a train."

"Gotcha."

## WESTIN HAWKINS, PART TWO

Westin never worked a day as a drover. After putting himself at risk to aid the scion of Kansas City's Sicilian mob family, his life had unexpectedly turned left at a fork in the road. His tattered clothes were replaced by tailored clothes in keeping with those worn by the young mobster, who truly considered himself a businessman, though his varied business interests leaned heavy toward the seedier side of life – the gambling operations, brothels, billiard parlors, tattoo parlors, loan sharking and any location serving liquor – Tommy understood human desire and was merely meeting those needs. With a nose for money, he innately appreciated supply and demand, pure and simple, with the occasional insertion of persuasion.

Over the next four years Westin spent most of his working time existing silently at Tommy's side. At first blush, he was an unimposing muscle man whose reputation for brutality spread by whispered rumor that inflated with each telling, fueled by the beatdown of the three thugs and the sporadic scuffle in which, for business purposes, he was forced to engage.

Westin himself, not unaware of the renown that preceded him, did nothing to dissuade its growth, yet volunteered almost nothing of himself. To his knowledge, none knew of his valor at the Battle of San Juan Heights, though he grasped how speaking of it would only enhance his growing notoriety. Friendly probing questions of his history over drinks were deftly deflected. The cowboy was modest to a fault. Westin grew in that direction, too.

On a late summer day in 1902 Tommy suggested a change in their mostly uneventful routine of making rounds in the several blocks surrounding the Union Depot and random locations adjacent to the stockyards. Unbeknownst to Westin, Tommy's father had dipped his toes into the quickly expanding collection of businesses feeding the industrial building expansion at the north end of the West Bottoms.

On that late summer day, the two men paid a call to Josiah Smith, a noticeably nervous middle-aged owner of Kansas River Sand and Gravel, a relatively new business located a little distance north of the stockyards along the Kansas River. Not shared with Westin was Tommy's father's silent partnership in the business, having stepped in less than a year after its founding with a substantial infusion of cash needed by Smith to keep his business, his life savings, from certain bankruptcy. Now, the ship seemingly righted, the local mobster boss had grown suspicious his investment wasn't yielding what it should and wanted someone loyal to be his eyes and ears on the inside.

When the subject was broached over dinner a week earlier at the family home, Tommy immediately recommended Westin, his trusted associate. Tommy's father was surprised. Like many others, he assumed the quiet young Westin's beneficial skills were loyalty, fast fists, and the fearlessness to use them.

"There's no doubt, Father, that respect I'd not seen to this degree is shown to the two of us, more so than when I worked alone," Tommy agreed. But, he explained, his young friend, though he spoke little and chose his words carefully, from time to time would suggest a subtle change which, invariably, resulted in improved tribute, increased earnings, more money.

"He's sharp as a tack and has a nose for money."

The late summer meeting with the wary Smith was actually one to introduce him to his new right-hand man, though Westin was still in the dark regarding the plan. Smith had been briefed on the plan at his home the preceding evening by two of Tommy's less subtle associates and was understandably resistant, but with unstated persuasion he relented and agreed to complete access by Westin to the business books and operations.

Breaking the news to Westin was left to Tommy. After the meeting with Smith, the two retreated to an upscale restaurant near the Union Depot where Tommy made the pitch. Westin was initially unsure of the proposal, though once he'd satisfied himself the change was a sign of respect and increased trust by the family, he warmed to the challenge the opportunity presented.

Bright and early the next morning Tommy and Westin showed up together at the sand and gravel company's little clapboard office building to finalize the hand-off. The rest of Westin's long day was spent meeting the dozen or so employees, beginning the daunting task of reviewing bank statements, invoices, contracts and other financial records. Stacks of pages with a whole lot of columns and way too many numbers, and many more pages filled with tons of words.

It was all a blur for Westin and later, upon reflection, he strongly suspected the seemingly helpful Smith might actually have intended to bury his new operating partner in such a deluge of intimidating numbers and words Westin might defer the details of the operation to the man who'd literally sold his nearby family farm to create a business ostensibly struggling to generate the expected profits. It worked.

On day two Westin showed up not in his tailored suit and shined shoes, but in the same tattered clothes he wore four years earlier when he hopped down from the empty boxcar. Westin immediately sought out Stefan Kajlich, the broad-shouldered Slav, the yard supervisor.

"Put me to work, Stefan," Westin said.

Kajlich eyed Westin suspiciously, then answered with a thick accent. "Very well, take a shovel, help load that wagon."

And so began Westin's career as a West Bottoms businessman. Though his laborer co-workers initially shunned him, their wariness over the new co-manager's motives gradually melted away as he worked as hard as any, never begging off or exerting privilege. They sweated, he sweated. They bitched, he listened.

In time, Westin became friendly with employees of wholesalers, employees of commodity purchasers, employees of a competitor. He learned about supply chains and transport. On occasion, an exhausted Westin relaxed over steak and a beer with Tommy, sharing the latest of what he'd learned of the business and his ever-evolving thoughts about missed opportunities and how it might be made to thrive.

Several months after his insertion at Kansas River Sand and Gravel, his knowledge concerning the business greatly enhanced, Westin was ready to return to the business office for a deep dive into the mountain of numbers and words that so overwhelmed him earlier.

Finally, confident in his assessment of the business, he met with Tommy on a late-May rainy day to share his thoughts. "Josiah is a terrible businessman," he said bluntly.

"Is he skimming?" Tommy asked, this being his father's primary concern.

"I'm certain he's not. He's strugglin', frazzled, prone to rash, illogical decisions. I'm equally certain I could easily double, triple our profits," Westin said.

Westin offered several examples of immediate expense reduction that would have no impact on the business gross revenues, starting with a reduction of the workforce by twenty-five percent and a slight change in the workday to better align with the contractor customers. "There's way too much standing around. Smith ignores his yard supervisor. He doesn't respect the ideas of others." He enthusiastically described how the business might increase its operating margin over the long-term by owning its supply chain, through acquisition, development, or both.

Westin related details from the number of instances he'd surreptitiously surveilled Smith after hours, tailing him to his modest home near the edge of the Quality Hill neighborhood, lingering about the neighborhood, wandering and always moving. Westin ticked off what he'd observed away from the business site. "The man retires early, rides the trolley, regularly attends church, doesn't drink or womanize, doesn't gamble. Before bed he's often in his study doing what I assume is business paperwork."

"Very good," Tommy said. "I'll pass it along and get back with you."

Turns out the rainy day on which Tommy and Westin met to discuss Josiah Smith's stewardship of Kansas River Sand and Gravel was one in a string of rain-soaked days across eastern Kansas. The rain continued, and continued, and continued across the plains, the dry creek beds and coulees gushing water into the streams, which dumped rushing silt-laden water into the smaller rivers, which unloaded their overbank payloads into the Kansas River. Before the two men could meet again the Kansas River had burst from its banks, wreaking extensive havoc throughout the West Bottoms, significantly interrupting Kansas City's economic engine, halting future development of churches and schools within the vulnerable floodplain. Thereafter, Kansas City's de facto downtown would shift 200 feet upward atop the bluff to its east.

One casualty of the 1903 flood, among many, was the river-adjacent Kansas River Sand and Gravel. Excess product stored on-site was washed away, and product for which purchaser contracts existed was washed away. The small clapboard office was washed away. The business, operating on thin margin as it was, clearly wouldn't survive without a fresh infusion of cash, and Don Lozarro, Tommy's father, wasn't inclined to throw good money after bad.

Days later, after the flood waters had finally receded, Tommy and Westin stood together in ankle-deep thick muck surveying the carnage. "My father has an offer for you."

"Okay," Westin agreed. "I'll meet with him."

The meeting occurred over bitterly strong coffee on the porch of the elder Lozarro's pleasant home. The old man explained his handshake loan to Smith would be called immediately. Smith would execute a deed transferring ownership of the business property to Westin, the Lozarro family would provide funding to cover existing obligations, re-build the site and short-term inventory, and for purchase of wholesaler product. The family would continue as a silent partner. Finally, Smith would be given a small sum of cash to help the former farmer with a fresh start.

Westin had anticipated this might be the offer, but he'd been unable to game it out long-term as anything other than an industrial version of sharecropping. By this time, he had lofty goals for himself, and appreciative as he might be for the trust placed in him, accepting the offer, he was convinced, would hobble his pursuit of wealth and respect.

"Thank you, Don Lozarro, for the trust you've shown in me, and for your respect," Westin said, faithfully repeating his rehearsed words, "and your generous offer. But I will accept, um, a different proposal."

The old man considered whether to feel slighted, but blew past the fleeting thought, finding it more than a bit refreshing to discuss business with a respectful, clear-thinking man not afraid to push back when most others would've feared to do so. With minor give-and-take, a handshake deal was reached. The financing would be repaid within ten years, and tribute would be paid for contracts secured with assistance from the family.

Westin, aided by yard supervisor Stefan Kajlich and a slimmed-down workforce, set to work straightaway building from the ground up the business he'd come to envision. The new office building was given a larger footprint and was constructed with brick and mortar. Westin unofficially christened its completion with his only Rough Rider keepsakes, tracking down a hammer and several nails from the yard, driving the nails partway into his office wall, looping his signature Rough Rider handkerchief over one nail and balancing his sheathed Rough Rider Bowie knife across the others. Finally, he attached his name to the company so all would know with whom they were doing business: Hawkins Sand and Gravel.

Within three years of launching Hawkins Sand and Gravel, in quick succession and made possible by wise management of his cashflow, Westin purchased a struggling quarry a few miles west of the metro area on a bluff overlooking the Kansas River, and a bit further west 20 acres of bottomland for sand harvesting. Also, he launched a small construction company focused on sub-work, started a lumberyard, and with his new transportation company - an early adopter of motorized transport - from raw material to a finished structure Westin was in line to profit from the West Bottoms' post-flood expansion into an industrial hub complimenting its livestock and meat-packing industries. Within five years his debt to Don Lozarro was repaid.

Shortly after his business empire had started to grow Westin set his sights on a wife and family. Recognizing his functional social skills would require a smidge of polishing, Westin sought out instruction on etiquette and ballroom dancing, made friends with the financial community leaders and leading politicians, and joined a Masonic lodge. Loyal to a fault, perhaps, at least one evening each month Westin dined with his only close friend, Tommy Lozarro.

Four years after creating Hawkins Sand and Gravel, well on his way toward his goals of success and wealth, Westin arrived at a church social and saw the most beautiful woman he'd ever seen, the woman he determined right then and there to marry. Seven years younger than Westin, with emerald green eyes and flowing auburn hair, Molly Burke was the middle daughter of a Kansas City banker. By the end of the evening, she was intrigued. Less than a year later, the couple was married in the growing city's social event of the year.

Nine months after returning from their two-week Estes Park honeymoon, Molly struggled giving birth at home to baby Gabriel.

There were complications following the baby's early morning birth. The concerned midwife screamed for Westin to bring the doctor and be quick about it. Westin burst into the birthing room and, with one look at Molly's pale face, flew down the stairs, out the door, running full-out the two blocks to Doc Peterson's dark home, where Westin's non-stop pounding on the door awakened the kindly doctor and neighbors up and down their sleepy street.

Westin and Doc Peterson hurried back as quickly as the old man's legs would carry him. They rushed up the stairs and into the birthing room where Westin was greatly relieved to find a much less frenzied scene. Propped up with extra pillows, Molly and Baby Gabriel were resting, the swaddled, sleeping baby laying across Molly's chest, soothed by its gentle rise and fall. Molly's color had returned, her sisters and exhausted midwife were smiling, and the collection of blood-soaked cloths was no longer growing.

Doc Peterson directed everyone out of the room and performed his examination, appearing in the crowded hallway several minutes later to announce a false alarm. A few minutes later, instructions given, Doc Peterson was headed home through the still night.

After the ladies and Westin had cleaned up the room, Molly's sisters settled on shifts and bid Westin good night. The midwife, left alone with Westin and a sleeping Molly, settled into comfortable chair in a corner of the room, a small pile of fresh linens across her lap. The midwife's concern persisted, but she chose for the time being not to say anything lest she come across as unduly alarmist.

Westin, oblivious to the midwife's continuing concern, leaned back in his favorite rocker next to the bed, totally unable to take his eyes off his precious baby son. In that moment, next to his baby boy and the woman with whom he'd spend the rest of his life, Westin knew absolutely his life had reached its zenith.

Later the next day Stefan Kajlich, having learned of the birth, called at the home, accompanied by his oldest daughter, Marie, a diminutive, quiet, eighteen-year-old with short-cropped hair. As Westin's business holdings expanded, his original yard supervisor had remained at his side with regularly increasing responsibility. Now, director of operations, Kajlich wore a tie and tailored suits to work. The callouses on his hands were greatly diminished. The cramped home along the Kansas River his expanding family lost to the 1903 flood waters had been replaced by successively larger homes atop Strawberry Hill. He took great pride in knowing Westin didn't make a move without first seeking his thoughtful counsel.

Several months earlier over early morning coffee Kajlich pitched the idea of his eldest daughter working as the Hawkins family nanny once the baby arrived. With seven younger siblings, Kajlich reasoned, Marie already had years of unpaid experience. Plus, Kajlich added, Marie's honesty, grit and work ethic rivaled his own. Westin, thinking this young woman sounded just like a younger, female version of her father, loved the idea, but cautioned it would be wholly contingent on Molly agreeing, too. The two men agreed to give it a shot.

Westin opened the baby room's door and ushered in the shy Marie and her father. Molly, resting in bed, her curious sisters standing close by, smiled, then broke out in giggles as Marie, fearful even of making eye contact with the room full of strangers, suddenly burst to life, darting straight to the crib. She turned, beaming, silently seeking permission to hold the swathed Gabriel. Molly smiled, nodding.

In that moment, Molly and her sisters were sold. Marie would be the family nanny.

Two days later, Westin returned to work. Though Molly had continued to lose small amounts of blood, Doc Peterson assured Westin and Molly's dubious sisters additional minor bleeding was not unexpected. Not to worry, he assured the family.

It was a little before lunch when a horse and carriage raced into the sand and gravel yard, the driver leaping out, shouting for Westin to come quick. A short time later, Westin burst into the baby's room. Doc Peterson, blood-soaked linens scattered about his feet, feverishly tended to Molly, barking orders for clean linens and boiled water. Marie stood silently in the corner holding baby Gabriel, slowly swiveling back and forth. Molly, flat on her back, face drained of color, eyes fixed on the ceiling, shivered uncontrollably until the shivering slowed, and finally stopped as her body went visibly limp.

Doc Peterson leaned forward with his stethoscope, searching for even the faintest sign of life. Molly was gone.

Westin, Molly's sisters and Marie, all watched in disbelief as Doc Peterson gently closed Molly's eyelids, packed up his bag, said something sincerely felt that no one heard, and left the family to their grief.

Over the succeeding years Westin threw himself into his work, and his son. In short time following Molly's passing, Marie's bonding with baby Gabriel was complete, irreversible, transforming her from nanny to the only mother he would ever know, and into Westin's life partner, though never as a lover. As much as the three needed one another, each wanted the other.

Westin spared no expense lavishing on Gabriel and Marie the best of anything they might have wanted or needed. He showered Marie with jewelry, clothing, always the best. Marie was the firm taskmaster who made sure Gabriel's homework was done, grades were at the top of his class, and curfews were obeyed.

Though Westin required his son earn spending money by working summers and holidays as a yard worker at Hawkins Sand and Gravel, a percentage of which absolutely had to be set aside as savings, he made sure his boy received the best private education. The Harvard admission not only cost Westin a pretty penny donation to the snooty school's endowment fund, he also burned favors owed to him for the glowing letters of recommendation from influential politicians.

Most years, the tight family unit vacationed together in Colorado, New York City, the Northwest, but the most memorable was their thirty-day trip to Europe when Gabriel was fifteen years old. London, Paris to Munich to Vienna by rail. At Vienna they boarded a luxury cabin cruiser chartered by Westin for a trip down the scenic Danube River to the historic city of Bratislava, capital of Czechoslovakia's Slovak region and home to Marie's uncle - her father's older brother - and a collection of cousins Marie had not seen since setting off for America as a little girl.

In the nearby tiny village of Baka, Marie's customarily stoic outward appearance melted away, and tears streamed down her face as they turned the corner of an ancient cobblestone street and she spied the picturesque cottage in which she was born. It was smaller than she remembered, but that mattered not a bit as she led Westin and Gabriel from one memory to another inside the home and about the well-tended yard. The cottage's current residents, complete strangers, were totally charmed by Marie's ebullient retelling of wonderful childhood memories long since buried away. After a long goodbye, with warm hugs and handshakes, the three trekked a short distance to the village church and its cemetery, where the family lingered until dusk at the graves of Marie's ancestors.

Reflecting later on the Europe trip, Westin was certain his growing son reaped benefit from it, whether the boy appreciated it in the moment or not. But more impactful was how it exposed to the driven, often single-minded businessman the complete Marie, revealing a piece of her he'd never seen, never dreamed existed. Westin didn't question their bond, but from that time forward he knew it was unbreakable.

## TUESDAY, JULY 10, 1934, EVENING

$B$eyond his tavern's regulars, like the quiet local couple that always took a table in the corner, the dusty, sweaty working stiffs who arrived after a hard days' work for a drink or two before heading home for supper, and the alkie who stumbled out onto a deserted sidewalk three or four nights a week, over time Augie Lenherr had honed his intuitive skill of judging a man at first sight. He could spot right away the local heat with his ill-fitting cheap suit and worn shoes, the college-educated businessman with his air of superiority, the out-of-town salesman wearing a rumpled suit and looking for a drink or two, or maybe a hook-up, and, on rare occasions, the mobster with his silk tie, spit-shined shoes and big city, tailored suit.

Augie knew right away his Tuesday night guest was a mobster, though thought it odd the well-groomed young man entered the half-filled River City Bar alone. These guys almost never travelled alone.

Out of the corner of his eye Augie watched as the dark-haired man paused inside the front door and casually adjusted one of his gold cuff links as he scanned the dimly lit bar, then saw him stride with purpose to the far side of the room and an empty table near one where Glenda was laughing with another of the regular working girls. Business was slow that evening and the girls were taking some time to catch up.

Paul made eye contact with Augie. "Club soda," Paul said loud enough for Augie to hear, and then motioned to Glenda's table for Augie to refresh their drinks.

Augie nodded, flipped the bar towel over his shoulder, mixed the women's drinks and carried them over, along with Paul's club soda, a napkin and bowl of peanuts.

Glenda and her friend looked up with surprise when the drinks arrived, but Augie merely flicked his head toward Paul. The women quickly swiveled in their chairs to see who was buying their drinks. After handing Augie a rolled-up twenty, Paul looked over and smiled at the local working girls and lifted his club soda in a toast to the two. The women grabbed their drinks and settled in at Paul's table.

"Evening, ladies," Paul said as he slid a twenty across the table to Glenda's friend. "I'd like to speak to Glenda. Alone."

The women looked at each other. "It's okay, Nancy," Glenda said, smiling back at Paul. "I'm okay."

Nancy picked up the twenty and her drink and retreated to Augie and the far end of the bar.

"So, mister . . . uh?" Glenda asked, raising a thin, lightly highlighted eyebrow.

"Paul. My name is Paul"

"And, where'd you get my name . . . Paul?"

Paul smiled. "Look, I just need a little information. Nothing else."

Paul leaned back and fished a money clip from his pants pocket, quickly peeling off five twenties that he dropped on the table in front of Glenda. She eyed the cash, but didn't reach for the bills.

"Gabriel Hawkins. His car was stolen. Just tell me what you know."

Glenda stared at the stranger. "You're not a cop," she said with certainty and an unmistakable southern drawl. "Who are you? And where you from? You're not from here? Wisconsin? No, Chicago. You from Chicago?"

"I'm a business associate of Mr. Hawkins," Paul answered.

"Ohhh, okay," Glenda said, well aware of the 'business associate' code.

In the time she'd been working as a prostitute to help support herself, her momma, and her fatherless toddler, Glenda considered herself fortunate not to have crossed paths with any of the local mobsters. She'd heard the terrifying stories of extortion, paying protection, vicious beatings of the girls who didn't pay, and the rapes. She didn't walk the streets and only worked her long-time friend Augie's back room and the backseat of a john's car. No hotel rooms, no john's house, and never, ever would she consider taking a john home with her. She finished her nights relatively early so she could get home to the small house she shared with her momma and still get enough sleep before heading down to the West Bottoms early the next morning to a grueling job at Loose-Wiles Biscuit Company. Raised frugally by a practical, single mother, Glenda had goals for herself and her son, and being a working girl was a means to a virtuous end.

Glenda reached forward and picked up the twenties, which she folded and put in her cheap pocketbook. "Whadda ya want to know?" she asked.

"Let's start with the theft of Hawkins' car."

Glenda related in detail, as best she could recall, how her friend Betty Jean hurried back into the tavern three nights earlier at 10:00 p.m. or so, and made a beeline to the table where Hawkins and Glenda were talking, sharing drinks. "She was in a huff," Glenda added for emphasis. She described how Hawkins flew out of his chair and ran to the door. She told Paul she followed Hawkins outside, but by the time she'd reached the sidewalk he was running back from the small parking area next to the tavern.

"His face was sweatin'. He looked like he'd seen a ghost." Glenda said.

Glenda described how she did her best to calm down the anxious businessman, pacing back and forth, head in hands, mumbling to himself, and finally convinced him to return inside where the two talked to Augie. She said Augie pleaded with Hawkins to call the police and report the theft, but he was adamant the cops not be involved.

"He kept looking at his watch," Glenda added. "Finally, Betty Jean – she's got a car – Betty Jean and me gave Mr. Hawkins a ride home and dropped him off. That's the last I've seen or heard of him."

"Who would he turn to if he needed help?" Paul asked.

The question stumped Glenda. "I dunno. Whadda ya mean?"

Paul was patient. "If he were on the lam, who would he call?"

"His rich daddy?" Glenda still wasn't sure what the mobster wanted from her.

"Would he call you?"

Glenda stared at Paul, wanting to laugh, but also not wanting to do something that might piss him off. "No, he wouldn't call me," she said flatly.

"The two of you ain't got anything going?" Paul asked. "He got a girlfriend? Boyfriend?"

Glenda could feel her eastern Kentucky blood start to boil. "Look, mister, not that it's any of your business, but Mr. Hawkins is, well, kind of a friend. A nice man. A lonely man. He comes in several times a week, we talk. We have a couple drinks. Nothin' else. Does he have a girlfriend? A boyfriend? I don't know, and I wouldn't tell a creep like you, no matter how much you paid me." Glenda leaned back, crossed her arms and stared at the young mobster. "We're done."

"You're right, Glenda. My apologies. I went too far." Paul pulled a pen from his shirt pocket and wrote the telephone number for Tallman's on a paper napkin. He wrapped another twenty around it and slid it over to Glenda. "I'm just trying to help our mutual friend. If you see him, hear from him, learn anything, please call this number. Ask for Vinny. I'll make it worth your while."

Paul pushed his chair back from the table, stood and nodded to Glenda as he turned to leave, but then turned back. "When the two of you talk and drink together, does Hawkins pay you?"

"Time is money, mister. Yes, he pays me."

Paul smiled. "Of course. Good evening, Glenda."

Glenda watched the mobster cross the room and leave the tavern. She turned in her chair and looked at Augie, who'd been watching from behind the bar.

Outside the tavern Paul walked briskly across the street to Vinny and the waiting Ford. After sliding into the passenger seat, he exhaled and loosened his silk tie.

"Find out anything?" Vinny asked.

"Well, yeah," Paul responded. "I don't think we're being double-crossed. Our boy is scared, but we knew that. Doesn't look like he's goin' into business for himself. He didn't want to tell the cops about his car being stolen."

"Overruled by daddy?" Vinny suggested.

"Could be."

"Whadda ya wanna do with the dame?" Vinny asked.

"It's a little late to drive out to bum-fuck Kansas lookin' for his car, so let's wait and follow her home. Find out where she lives." Paul looked over at Vinny. "Got enough smokes, Vinny? We might be there awhile."

"Hang on, Paul. That her?" Vinny pointed at a slim redhead leaving the tavern alone.

"Yeah, that's her."

The two men watched as Glenda turned and walked away from them, passing a parked car before crossing the poorly lit street to a sidewalk on the opposite side. A bit further she turned at the corner and disappeared behind a mangle of untrimmed shrubbery.

"Looks like she's hoofing it, Vinny. Let's keep our distance. Find out where she goes."

Vinny started the Ford's engine and pulled away from the curb, crawling slowly forward.

"Cut the lights, Vinny. Stay a block back."

A couple of blocks later Glenda crossed the street mid-block and walked up the steps to the covered porch of a darkened bungalow. Vinny eased the Ford to the curb half a block back and cut the engine. The men watched as Glenda opened the front door and went inside. Almost immediately a room at the front of the single-story home lit up behind pulled curtains. The men could make out Glenda's silhouette as she moved across the room. Vinny fished out his matches and fired up a Lucky Strike.

As Paul and Glenda spoke, not far away on the other side of downtown Kansas City, Kansas, a famished Diehl sat alone in a booth at O'Grady's Pub nursing a warm Pabst while waiting for his ham-on-rye sandwich. He tried piecing together the events of the day but kept returning to his latest interaction with Detective Brandt. Something doesn't fit with this guy, Diehl thought. He was startled when an unexpected hand gripped the top of his shoulder. Looking up, Diehl was surprised to see the smiling face of the department's gregarious police chief, Harold "Big Hal" Finney, accompanied by his wife. The couple was dressed for something fancy, something requiring silk ties, real pearls and matching earrings.

"Detective Diehl, a pleasure to see you," Finney said.

"Thanks, Chief. Great to see you, too," Diehl said, nodding to the Chief's wife. "Just trying to piece some things together on that car theft case."

Finney didn't respond but turned to his wife. "Dear, please let me speak to the detective for a moment. We won't be late."

After his wife left the two, Finney slid into the booth opposite Diehl.

"So, Detective Diehl, let's chat about this car theft case."

As Glenda approached her home she was concerned to see it unusually dark. No lights burned. Not even the front porch light. Not like her momma at all, Glenda thought. After the disturbing conversation she'd just had with a man she was certain was a real-life mobster, the dark house was alarming.

Glenda did her best to walk lightly across the wood-plank steps and porch and listened for a moment at the front door. It was dead silent along Glenda's working-class neighborhood street, and she heard nothing from inside the house. She slowly turned the door handle and gently leaned her shoulder against the solid wood door, but it didn't budge. The deadbolt was locked.

In the dark Glenda fished around in her purse for the house keys, then slowly, quietly inserted the key and unlocked the door.

Glenda had opened the front door but a few inches before she heard her mother's voice, not much louder than a whisper. "We're in here, dear."

Glenda stepped into the house and quickly shut the door behind her, instinctively locking the deadbolt behind her. Her hand found the light switch on the wall. "Oh, my God," she said as she dropped her purse, mouth wide open as she stared at her momma and snoozing little boy, and a grimy Gabriel Hawkins sharing space on the bare wood floor against a living room wall. "What, what . . . ?" Glenda searched for a question, then hurried across the room to her baby boy. She turned and looked at Hawkins.

Hawkins held a forefinger to his lips. "It's okay, Glenda. Your boy's okay." He looked at her momma. "Your mother's okay. I've given her a little background." Hawkins paused, before adding. "I'm not okay."

"No fuck, shitlock," the smooth southern accent disintegrating into hardcore southern backwoods. Glenda stopped and calmed herself. "Not fifteen minutes ago I was talkin' to a gangster. A goddamned gangster. About you." She pointed at Hawkins. "Looking for you!" Glenda could feel the intensity rising within her. She looked at her momma and back at Hawkins. They were expressionless. Oh my God, Glenda realized. They're scared shitless.

Glenda sat down on the floor next to her momma. "What the fuck is goin' on, Mr. Hawkins?"

"Everyone sit tight," Hawkins said. "I'm just gonna kill the light."

Vinny leaned forward in his car seat. "There she goes, Paul . . . No, no, no, that's a man!"

Paul was watching too. It was brief, but the silhouette they saw rise near a side window of the house was definitely not Glenda. A couple of seconds after seeing the silhouette, the room went dark again.

"Okay, that was weird," Vinny said. "She married, Paul?"

"No idea, Vinny, but I doubt it. She's a whore. Besides," Paul added, "the stuff with the lights is odd."

"Yeah, that's kinda hokey," Vinny agreed. "I'm sure that was a man."

"Yeah, I think our boy's in there, Vinny."

"You sure, Paul?"

"No, I'm not sure at all. Just a hunch." Paul said. "If it's him, you gotta place we can take him?"

"Yeah, I gotta place," Vinny answered. "What's the plan?"

"I'll take the front door, Vinny. You go around back and grab him if he tries to run again."

Vinny pulled the Ford up to the curb opposite Glenda's home and shut off the engine. He checked his shouldered revolver and the two men left the car. Vinny walked quickly around the side of the house and disappeared in the darkness. Paul waited a few seconds before walking slowly up the steps and across the porch. He knocked several times on the door, firmly, slowly, and took a step back.

Paul heard muffled voices and movement inside the house, followed by illumination of the porch. He heard the deadbolt being unlocked. The door opened slowly, slightly. "Whadda ya doin' here, mister? Whadda ya want?"

"Glenda?"

"Whadda ya want? Are ya hard of hearin'?" Glenda was doing her best to stand up to the mobster, but she was shaking inside. Every cell in her body screamed out in fear.

"Just send Mr. Hawkins out and I'll be on my way. I just wanna talk to him."

Before Glenda could respond, there was a loud commotion along the side of house. Paul shot across the porch to see Vinny with Hawkins in a head-lock, half-dragging him toward the street. "This him?" Vinny asked as Hawkins struggled.

Paul jumped off the porch and grabbed Hawkins' curly hair, jerking his head back. "Yeah, that's him." Paul said, looking back at the porch in time to see the door close. "Let's get outta here."

Glenda rushed to the window, watching in horror as the two mobsters dragged a struggling Hawkins to their car before pushing him to the street. After a quick flurry of punches by both, they jerked him to his feet and pushed him into the back seat of the Ford. Paul climbed in with Hawkins, slammed the door shut and the car roared off down the street. It all took but a few seconds, but for Glenda peeking out, it was a shockingly surreal scene. In that moment she knew she'd never again see the kind Mr. Hawkins. It was like watching his sudden murder on the street in front of her home.

Glenda stepped out onto the porch as the car sped down the street. She flew back into the house, frantically feeling in the dark for the light switch. Flipping on the light she screamed at her frightened mother, "We gotta go, let's go, let's go!"

Glenda's mother, huddling against the far wall next to her grandbaby, scrambled to her feet. "Slow down, dear," she said, reaching her hysterical daughter and grabbing her shoulders. Tears started rolling down Glenda's cheeks as she broke down sobbing in her mother's arms. "It's okay, dear. Talk to me."

Glenda pulled away and wiped her face with a clenched fist, focused again. "We gotta go momma. They're gonna kill Mr. Hawkins. They've got Mr. Hawkins and they're gonna kill him. They'll kill us, too. We gotta go."

Glenda sent her mother to the bedroom, telling her to pack a bag as fast as possible. She hurried across the room to where she'd left her purse, plopped down and emptied it onto the floor between her legs. She frantically flipped through the contents until she found Diehl's business card. Leaving the mess behind she scrambled to her feet and ran back to the kitchen and the telephone that hung from the wall. She dialed the number on Diehl's card, tapping her foot impatiently as she waited for an answer.

"Police. This is Brandt, Detective Brandt."

Glenda paused. Brandt broke the silence. "Hullo. Speak or I'm hangin' up," he barked.

"Wait, wait," Glenda blurted out. "Is Detective Diehl there?"

"Nope, just me. Whadda ya want me to tell him, lady?"

"Well, tell him Glenda called. It's really, really important. Tell him they've got Mr. Hawkins." Glenda paused. She hadn't thought where the family would flee. "Tell him to meet me where we were talkin'."

Brandt scribbled a line of notes. "You gotta last name lady?"

"Glenda. Just Glenda," and she hung up, flying back out to the living room to find a suitcase in the middle of the room, and her mother holding the dozing toddler.

Glenda picked up the suitcase. "C'mon momma, we gotta go. It ain't far."

## TUESDAY, JULY 10, 1934, LATE EVENING

Vinny stomped on the gas and the Ford roared away from Glenda's quiet neighborhood. In the back seat Hawkins was bent over, sobbing inconsolably as Paul struggled to land a solid punch to the head. "Stop the cryin' you fuckin' bitch, you little baby," he yelled, before throwing another flurry of punches. He grabbed Hawkins by the hair and jerked him upright, slapping him several times. "Shut up, shut up, shut up," Paul screamed. "Shut up, I'm not gonna kill you." He pushed Hawkins' head down between his legs, waiting for the sobbing to end.

Hawkins slowly gathered control of himself. "Where you taking me?"

Paul stopped pushing down on Hawkins' head and leaned back in the car seat. "Sit up, Gabe." Paul waited for Hawkins to raise up, then handed him a handkerchief. "You're a mess, Gabe. Clean your face."

Hawkins wiped away tears and blew his nose. "Where you taking me, Paul?"

The mobster ignored the question. He was pissed at the mess he was having to deal with. "Remember that small dorm room at Harvard, Gabe? You always had to have your way. Too damn smart for your own good. Never wanted to listen, did you?"

Over the past several days Paul couldn't help but think of the odd, otherwise unlikely friendship created by chance when a mobster's kid and a Midwestern rich kid were thrown together as Harvard freshmen roomies. Money and influence got each admitted, but each soon figured out no amount of money or influence would buy their admittance into the old-money cliques on campus. They were no better than the faceless help to their east coast, prep-school classmates. Paul a Guido, a wop, and Hawkins the offspring of a Cowtown millionaire.

Along with a handful of other campus outcasts, Paul and Hawkins created a tight-knit group of friends who supported each other and stayed in touch after their undergrad days. More often than not it was Hawkins who reached out to the others. Christmas and birthday cards, weddings, the occasional call or telegram. And, it was Hawkins, ever chasing the big score, who visited Chicago for lunch with Paul to pitch a "can't miss" job.

Paul had listened with an open mind to Hawkins' scheme. Hawkins had considered every detail, even suggesting they find a forger outside the United States. He showed the young gangster a legit bond and unfolded the piece of paper Beasley had used to recreate the government officials' signatures. He laid the paper next to the bond. "Check that out, Paul. Identical."

As Paul listened to Hawkins' pitch, front of mind was the caution of his father to keep friendships at arm's length from business, their business, because the unintended consequences might lead to much worse than hurt feelings.

"Gabe, your idea just might work," Paul told his friend, "but you know what I do, what my father does, and I promise, you don't wanna do business with us. It's for your own good." Patiently, Paul explained to his friend that a scheme like his would almost certainly blow up, and when that occurred the collateral damage, who got hurt, who got sacrificed, would be out of his hands.

"Drop it, Gabe, or at least the thought of doing it with me."

But Hawkins was a persistent salesman, confident and unconcerned with Paul's warnings. Finally, satisfied he'd done what he could to dissuade his friend, Paul agreed to run it up the flagpole and get back in touch. Not surprisingly, his father and Ricitti liked the idea straight away. With a degree or two of separation it was a no-brainer. The elder Bunicci pressed his youngest son. "Does your friend understand our business, our loyalties?"

"He does, pops. He knows enough. I did my best to get him to walk away."

The old man looked at Ricitti, then back at Paul. "Very good. He's a grown boy. Let's get started on this straight away." Tony directed Ricitti to reach out to an associate in Toronto who could track down a Frenchman most considered the best paperhanger in North America. "He was doing time, but I heard some time ago he's out."

Tony continued. "Angelo, we'll need someone close to push the bonds." Tony rubbed his chin. "Give me a second, his name'll come to me." The three men sat in silence for a moment until the old man raised a forefinger. "Doolittle. Tom? No, Ted Doolittle. Works in a brokerage downtown. He owes us a favor."

Tony thought for a moment before speaking again. "Okay, Paul, get the list of serial numbers and denominations. Angelo, visit Mr. Doolittle's firm and purchase one bond of each denomination. We'll send all to our man up in Canada. Don't speak to Mr. Doolittle until we have finished product back from Kansas City. We'll hook him by calling in our favor and having him push out one or two of the bonds back to Mr. Hawkins, then amp it up from there after the hook's been set."

Ricitti turned to Paul. "Who does the signatures?"

"Hawkins wouldn't tell me. He says the guy doesn't know about us, either. Says he'll keep his yap shut."

Hawkins had stopped whimpering by the time the Ford crossed the Missouri River into North Kansas City. Paul leaned over and draped an arm over Hawkins' shoulders, raising his chin with a forefinger. "Hey, you've screwed up Gabe. You know that, right? Got the coppers involved."

"I know, I know. I'm sorry, I'm so, so sorry."

"It's okay, Gabe. The three of us - you, me, Vinny - we're gonna figure out how to clean it up. Keep us out of trouble." Paul gave Hawkins a quick hug. "You with me, Gabe? Huh?" Paul looked up at the rearview mirror and made eye contact with Vinny.

Hawkins nodded. "I'm with you, Paul."

Vinny took the first exit after crossing the river and dropped down to an old river road on which settlers had first traveled. Unpaved after a short distance, the road's current condition wasn't much better. Dodging ruts in the narrow, tree-lined lane, the Ford drove for only a few minutes before making a sharp turn, stopping in front of a closed gate. A short distance ahead in the darkness a solitary light burned in the window of a decent-size, rusty metal building. Elsewhere about the property on either side of the drive toward the building the silhouettes of discarded cars, tractors and other metal equipment created an eerie, spooky environment. Beyond the back side of the salvage yard flowed the mighty Missouri River.

Two German Shepherds, barking and growling, came running from the darkness toward the gate. A hunched-over figure passed by the building's lighted window and, within a moment, was walking slowly toward the gate.

"It's old man Lazia," Vinny said, then flashed the Ford's headlights.

The faithful senior unlocked the gate and pulled it open, then walked to the car's driver's side. Vinny leaned out the window. "Good evening, Mr. Lazia. We'll need you to close the gate behind us and take a walk. Maybe a couple hours."

The old man nodded and stepped back as the Ford pulled forward. Vinny drove slowly along the uneven drive, following it to the backside of the building where an even larger area was completely filled with even more rusty metal junk. Cottonwoods lined the far end of the yard, separating it from the river. Vinny parked the car next to a truck backed up to a loading dock. "The door's over there," Vinny said, pointing.

Vinny led the way inside the building's shop area. They skirted a mostly broken-down car surrounded by wood stools and various tools left behind earlier in the evening by workers tearing it down for its parts. Beyond, Vinny led them to the only open space in the shop. He walked over to a desk set against the wall and grabbed a metal chair, dragging it across the hard-packed dirt floor. Vinny set it in the middle of the open area. "Have a seat, Gabe," Paul directed.

Hawkins shot a questioning glance at Paul, then at Vinny, then stepped forward and slowly seated himself in the chair. Paul moved forward, kneeling down in front of Hawkins as Vinny walked to the back side of the room. "You want a smoke, Gabe?" Paul asked.

"No, no thank you."

Paul looked over Hawkins' shoulder as Vinny returned with a few strands of wire. "Put your hands behind the chair, Gabe?" Paul said.

Hawkins turned and looked at Vinny, then back at Paul. "What? Why?"

"It's for your own good, Gabe. Nothing to worry about," Paul said as Vinny tied Hawkins' hands together, twisting the wire tight, making Hawkins flinch. Vinny stepped around the chair, knelt down and secured Hawkins' legs to the chair. "Thank you, Vinny," Paul said as the hefty gangster stood and backed a few steps away.

"We're just gonna have a conversation, Gabe," Paul said calmly.

Sweat was beading on Hawkins' forehead. At that moment he knew, despite Paul's calm voice and demeanor, he wouldn't leave the building alive. "Please don't kill me, Paul," he begged. Hawkins dropped his head and started sobbing softly.

Paul stood and looked at Vinny, then knelt back down in front of his college roomie. "There, there, Gabe, calm down, stop crying," Paul said as he took out his handkerchief and dabbed at the tears streaming down Hawkins' face. "I'm not gonna kill you."

Paul stepped over and grabbed a stool, setting it down in front of Hawkins. Paul squatted down onto the stool and stared at his friend. "You back with me, Gabe?"

Hawkins nodded.

"Okay, Gabe, where are my bonds? You missed the train."

Hawkins took a moment to summon the courage, then succinctly described the evening at Augie's and learning his car was stolen. "I panicked, Paul."

Paul smiled and patted Hawkins on the cheek. "It's okay, Gabe. It's okay. So, the bonds are in the car?"

"Yeah, but they're hidden."

"Hidden?" Paul asked. "Whadda ya mean?"

Hawkins described how he'd paid a mechanic on the Missouri side to create a secret compartment in the car once the scheme started and he knew he'd be running the bonds. "I didn't want the coppers to find 'em if they ever stopped me. Wasn't thinkin' of someone stealing the car. But, no one's finding 'em unless they know where to look."

Paul thought for a moment. "So, Gabe, if we find the car, do we find the bonds?"

"Yeah, prob'ly so. Cops are looking for it. Got their best guy on it. Dad called in a favor for me."

Paul smiled. "Mmm, so it would seem."

"Tell me about your secret compartment, Gabe." Hawkins responded straight away, describing where the compartment was located, and the trick to accessing it.

"That helps, Gabe. You're doing great. Now, tell me everyone who knows anything about the dirty bonds and what we're doing with 'em?"

Hawkins answered immediately, blurting, "No one."

Paul smiled and looked at Vinny, who'd taken a chair a few steps behind and to the side of Hawkins. Paul looked back at Hawkins. "Now, Gabe, I need you to think before answering. Take your time. This is important for all of us, including you. So, let's try again. Who knows?"

Hawkins was silent for a moment. "No one, Paul. I kept my mouth shut."

"Okay, okay, Gabe, what about your old man?" Paul asked. "Vinny tells me the boys here in KC have done some work with him. He know anything about the bonds? Share it with dad?"

"No, Paul, he doesn't know anything."

Paul gave Vinny a knowing look and a nod.

"The housekeeper? She know anything?"

"Who?" Paul asked, confused.

"Your maid, Gabe. She introduced Vinny to her double-barrel." Paul smiled as Vinny let loose with a belly laugh.

"Oh, her," Paul said, shaking his head. "No, she doesn't know anything."

"What about your whore girlfriend?"

It took Hawkins a moment to realize the mobster was asking about Glenda. "Oh, heck no. Jeepers, Paul, she's not my girlfriend. We just talk. I pay her to talk to me."

Vinny snorted, laughing. "That's pretty fuckin' sad."

"So, Gabe, what about the guy who signs the bonds? He knows something, doesn't he?"

Hawkins chose his words carefully. "He knows me, he knows he gets cash for doing it, and he knows not to spend his money or say anything to anyone. You don't need to worry about him."

"Who is he, Gabe?"

Lips trembling, Hawkins didn't respond. In that moment it struck him his father and the rest were on Paul's hit list. They were dead as sure as he was going to be dead.

"C'mon, Gabe, it's gonna be morning before we get you home. Who's the guy? Where's he live?"

Hawkins didn't answer.

Paul stood up slowly and looked at Vinny. "I don't want my friend going home with a bloody nose, Vinny."

The hulking Kansas City mobster removed his suitcoat and draped it over the back of a chair, then walked slowly around to Hawkins's right side. Hawkins looked up at Vinny. When their eyes met the big man planted and threw a right to Hawkins' gut. Hawkins didn't notice the chair skid backward several inches. His soft torso was no match for Vinny's meaty fist, seemingly reaching all the way to Hawkins' spine, leaving him doubled over and gasping for air.

Vinny looked at Paul, who waved him off and stepped back in front of Hawkins. "Gabe, I'm trying to protect you here, and I'll be as honest as I can. See, we need to deal with this guy who's been signing the bonds. No loose ends. Whether you help us or not, we're gonna find him. But, if you help us, you go home tonight. If not, well . . . ." Paul's voice trailed off. "Wise up, Gabe. Save yourself."

Hawkins stared at the floor. He had no doubt Paul would figure out how to find Beasley, and kill him, whether Hawkins spilled the beans or not. Paul had just made that crystal clear. Either way, Hawkins told himself, Beasley's a dead man. "Okay," Hawkins said. "I'll tell you what you need to know."

Paul knelt down again, but before he could say anything Hawkins made a last-ditch effort to save the rest. "They don't know nothin', Paul!"

Paul raised his hands. "Hands off, Gabe, you've got my word."

Desperate to believe Paul's sincerity, Hawkins launched into a rambling monologue about his friendship with Beasley, and how he'd sold his young friend on joining the scheme. With little hesitation he gave the two mobsters Beasley's boarding home address, a physical description, and the name of the fancy department store where he was working since being fired by the State Treasurer.

Paul weighed what Hawkins had told him, judging whether he'd been told the truth. Maybe Gabe was spinning a yarn to protect his friend? No, Paul thought, he's too frazzled to make it up. It all fits together, Paul thought: a lifelong friend, employee of the State Treasurer. Besides, the clock was ticking. "Gabe, months ago, you remember the warning I gave you about doing business with me? Remember?" Paul said calmly as he stood.

Hawkins stared at the floor, brow furrowed as he racked his brain. Hawkins' head shot up and he barely uttered "Oh shit," before Vinny, who'd moved quietly behind him, trained a towel-wrapped .22 revolver to the back of his head and pulled the trigger. A muffled "pop" resonated through the workshop. Hawkins' head flung forward, his terror-filled eyes staring blankly ahead. His body went limp and he tumbled sideways, toppling the chair.

Vinny stepped around the lifeless body and pressed the barrel of the towel-wrapped gun under Hawkins' breastbone. Another muffled "pop" reverberated through the workshop. One to the head, one to the heart. Paul watched without emotion as Vinny quickly searched Hawkins' pockets, pulling out his wallet and random scraps of paper before removing Hawkins' watch and a ring. Satisfied anything of value or quick identification was gone from the body, Vinny nodded toward a large rusty barrel in the corner of the workshop. "We'll stuff him in there, roll it onto the truck and drive it over to the river. Grab a crowbar and we'll poke a few holes in the barrel so it'll sink once it gets downstream a ways."

# WEST BOTTOMS

## TUESDAY, JULY 10, 1934, STILL LATE
## EVENING

Brandt sighed and hung up the telephone receiver. "Dames," he muttered under his breath. He scribbled a few more words and stood just as a sullen looking Diehl entered the room, his half-eaten ham-on-rye wrapped in a paper napkin. A brief, disturbing conversation with Chief Finney had turned his world upside down, leaving him more than a little shaken and seriously questioning those with whom he was working.

"Whadda ya doin' at my desk, Brandt?" a suspicious Diehl asked.

Brandt picked up the lined-page and scribbled notes. "A dame named Glenda just called for ya. Wouldn't give me her last name, but figure you don't need it, right?"

Diehl didn't answer, snatching the page from Brandt's hand. "I can't read any of this, Brandt. It's gibberish. What's it say?"

"She sounded frantic, scared. Says 'they've got 'Mr. Hawkins,' and she says she'll meet you where you were talkin' to her." Brandt paused as Diehl stared at the notes he couldn't decipher. "Make sense to you, Diehl?"

"Yes, yes," Diehl said quietly as he settled into his chair.

"You alright, Diehl?"

"Yes, I'm alright. Thank you, Brandt."

Diehl stood. He needed to keep moving. "I'll see you tomorrow, Brandt."

"Want a sidekick?"

Diehl considered the offer, then shook his head. "Thanks, but no. See ya tomorrow."

Diehl stood, reflexively patted his holstered gun, took a wolf-size bite of his sandwich, dropped the rest in a trash can and flashed a quick wave to Brandt as he hustled across the squad room. Taking the stairs two at a time he was out on the sidewalk and behind the wheel of his Studebaker in no time.

Flooring the engine Diehl headed east on Minnesota. A few blocks later he checked his mirrors as he cruised slowly past the River City. Diehl checked his mirrors again before pulling over to the curb a block down from the bar. Finally, satisfied he hadn't been followed, Diehl stepped onto the deserted street and strode past the bar, scanning the few scattered cars for anything out of place.

Certain the bar wasn't being staked out, Diehl backtracked to the bar's front door and pushed it open to see a smattering of late-night regulars and a concerned Augie behind the bar. Their eyes met. Augie nodded, motioning for Diehl to follow. The two walked quickly through the vacant kitchen and into a dark hallway, at the end of which was Augie's office. Augie stopped before reaching his office and knocked slowly, three times, on a door off the hallway. Three light knocks were made from the other side of the door.

Augie fished a key ring from his baggy pants, found the correct key and unlocked the door. Opening the door just a crack, he whispered, "Detective Diehl is here. He's alone." Augie motioned Diehl to come closer, then opened the door to reveal a tiny utility closet, grandmother and her sleeping grandson huddled together on the floor next to a mop bucket, Glenda protecting the two with a wood-handled plunger.

Diehl said calmly, "You can lower the weapon, Glenda. We're gonna get you someplace safe."

Diehl turned to Augie. "You got a back door?"

Augie nodded toward his office. "Through there. You can park out back."

"Okay, I'll pull around back. Get these three to the back door and wait for my signal. Three knocks."

Diehl spun around and retreated back through the bar and onto the street, again scanning the street. He fired up the Studebaker and pulled a U-turn, rushing up the street, through the bar's parking lot and up to a door on the bar's backside. Diehl jumped out and ran to the door, knocking three times. Immediately, Augie threw open the door and Glenda's momma hustled out, followed by Glenda and her now restless toddler.

"Passenger side, back seat, duck down," Diehl said quietly as the three rushed past him to the idling car. He glanced back at Augie who nodded as he closed and locked the door.

Diehl hurried around to the driver's side, shifted into gear and drove slowly around the bar to the street. He looked left and right before turning north toward Minnesota. "Okay folks, keep your heads down. We're going for a little drive."

After retracing his earlier route past city hall and police HQ, Diehl turned off the main drag and weaved his way on side streets back toward the River City, making right and left turns every block or so, constantly checking his rearview mirrors. Following several minutes of evasive driving, confident no one was tailing them, Diehl turned onto 7th Street and headed south down Strawberry Hill to the Kansas River floodplain, leaving the neighborhoods and streetlamps behind.

Crossing the Kansas River on a steel truss bridge, Glenda hollered from the back seat, "We going over to the Missouri side?"

"No, no, we're still in Kansas. After this hill we'll drop down to Southwest Boulevard. Not far from there."

A few minutes later Diehl turned off the well-traveled Southwest Boulevard into the working-class hamlet of Rosedale, a wooded town consumed years earlier by the metro area's urban sprawl and annexed into Kansas City, Kansas. He parked along the cut limestone curb of a compact home on a dark street. He turned and looked down at his passengers. "Stay down. I'll be right back."

Diehl stepped out of the car and walked quickly to a dark front porch, knocking lightly on the door. Within a moment the porch light came on and the wood door opened a crack. "Donkey poop!" Lulu cried out, the sound traveling down the street.

"Shh, shhh," Diehl exclaimed, gesturing for his little sister to bring it down a few decibels. "My goodness, you're gonna wake the dead," he smiled, before adding, "Dumbass."

"No, you're a dumbass," Lulu shot back, throwing open the door. "Come on in."

"Wait. I will, but I've got a huge, huge favor to ask. It's an emergency." He paused. "It's dangerous."

"Dangerous? Seriously?"

"Yeah, definitely dangerous."

"I'm in."

Diehl and his sister whispered back and forth for a few seconds before he returned to the Studebaker and his terrified passengers.

"Okay, Glenda, mom, chop-chop. Straight to the house and straight inside." He reached out. "Give me junior." Cradling the squirming toddler Diehl turned and led the ladies into his sister's cozy home.

"Shades down, Sis," Diehl ordered after shutting and locking the front door. "Lights to a minimum." He handed the toddler to Glenda, then did a quick audit of windows and the back door. Returning to the front of the home Diehl found Lulu sitting on a loveseat next to Glenda.

"Where we at, Detective Diehl?" Glenda asked.

Diehl motioned to his sister. "Well, Glenda, this is my sister, Lulu. Lulu, this is Glenda, mom, and, uh, Junior."

"Bobby Joe and Mary Jo," Glenda said, her southern drawl unmistakable.

Lulu smiled. "Welcome to my home, ladies."

Diehl spent the next thirty minutes interrogating Glenda about the evening's events. She started out frazzled and scattered in her recollection, but gradually calmed and became more focused. Diehl kept returning to the bar interaction and Hawkins' kidnapping, seeking clarifications and asking additional questions, extracting even more detail, feverishly recording notes on the pages of his pocket notepad. Lulu listened with rapt interest, hunched over, chin resting in her hands.

Finally, satisfied he had a complete picture from start to finish, Diehl laid down the rules to keep Glenda and family, and Lulu, as safe as possible: shades drawn at all times, no one except for Lulu outside, don't talk to anyone, don't answer the door for anyone. "Don't trust anyone but me."

"Coppers?" Lulu piped up.

"No one but me," Diehl shot back.

The seemingly chance conversation with Chief Finney earlier in the evening had thrown Diehl for a huge loop. The Chief's parting advice, even though given with his customary friendly smile and a fatherly pat on the shoulder, made him shudder. The puzzle pieces were starting to come together for Diehl. A completed puzzle, not so fast.

"One last thing, kiddo," Diehl said, reaching down to lift a cuffed pant and pull a small .22 caliber revolver from the holster strapped to his lower leg. "Don't touch the trigger and don't point it at anyone unless you intend to shoot," he said, handing it to Lulu. "Keep it with you at all times. Trust your sixth sense. It'll tell you if you might need to use it." He gently laid a thumb on the gun's hammer. "Hammer back, aim for the chest, shoot until there's no bullets left, scream and run as fast as you can. It's a double action, so all you gotta do is keep pulling the trigger." Their eyes met. "Got it?"

Lulu smiled. "I got it, donkey-poop."

Diehl smiled and rose. "Okay, I gotta get back to work. Glenda, mom, you guys good?"

The ladies nodded.

"I'll check in tomorrow morning. 'Jayhawk' will be the code word when I call." Diehl wheeled to leave, stopped and turned back. "Glenda, you're not working tomorrow. Lulu, you supposed to work at Macy's tomorrow?"

Lulu nodded.

"Okay, you need to be there. Mum's the word."

"Got it."

Diehl looked back at his little sister's mostly dark house before driving away. He circled back a couple minutes later, checking for bad guys. Nothing. Satisfied the women and little Bobby Joe were safe, he headed back to police HQ, arriving to a deserted detective squad room, save for the seemingly ever-present Detective Brandt.

"You ever sleep, Brandt?" Diehl asked as he plopped down at his desk.

Brandt pushed back from his desk, stood and started across the room toward Diehl, brushing food crumbs from his cheap tie and wrinkled dress shirt. "You wanna bring me up to speed?" Brandt asked as he pulled up a chair.

Diehl rubbed his chin. "It's a puzzle, Brandt. It centers on a rich boy and his shiny green Ford. Somehow, he's tied up with some gangsters, some real bad guys." Diehl paused. "I tellin' you anything you don't already know?"

"Gabriel Hawkins?" Brandt asked. "Daddy does sand and gravel, trucking, construction, a lot of shit?"

Diehl nodded.

"And who are the bad guys?"

Diehl considered the question for a moment. "I saw two of 'em high-tailin' it from Hawkins' home yesterday. The son's home." Diehl shared some of what he'd learned from Glenda that evening, but not everything.

"Where'd your hooker meet the bad guy?" Brandt asked.

"Glenda. Her name is Glenda. A joint on the Kansas side."

"Right, Glenda. Where'd you find her, pick her up?"

"At her house," Diehl lied.

"Where you got her stashed, Diehl?"

"Someplace safe," Diehl answered.

"Mr. Slick, the bad guy who scared the shit outta your hooker, er, Glenda, think he's local?"

Diehl leaned back. "Whoa, Brandt, where'd that come from?"

Brandt stood, checking his tie for food stains. "See ya in the morning, Diehl. Find the car, solve your puzzle."

"You must be exhausted," Lulu said, handing Glenda a glass of water.

Mary Jo and Bobby Joe were fast asleep down the hall in Lulu's bedroom, but Glenda was wide awake, afraid, and ready for a chance to lean on a friendly soul. "Yes," she finally answered, dabbing at her teary eyes with a clenched handkerchief. "Why do I always do the wrong thing?"

Lulu listened, sensing Glenda needed to unload a whole lot she'd bottled up. Glenda described being a small girl growing up in the eastern Kentucky Appalachians, in a cabin tucked away in a backwoods holler, with a coal miner daddy, a little brother, and her momma.

"Daddy liked me to sit on his knee when he strummed his guitar and sang to me. I wish I remembered more, but what I remember is good."

Glenda's daddy liked to drink a bit, Glenda's momma later confided, but never hit her, never hit the kids. One evening her daddy headed off to buy some 'shine and for whatever reason took along her little brother. The 'shine still exploded, killing her daddy, little brother, and two others.

The day following the funerals Glenda's mother bundled her and a few hurriedly packed bags onto a neighbor's horse-drawn wagon and they rode out of the holler, never to lay eyes on it again. Two days later her momma's cousin met them at Union Depot in the West Bottoms and brought them to her home on Strawberry Hill. In no time Glenda's momma was working as a domestic and, eventually, they found a home of their own.

"Lulu, it was my choice to quit school." She recounted how her momma's physical deterioration from the "shakes" had, at first, been minor, and the spells infrequent, but over time became more debilitating and more frequent. Her momma was finding it hard to stay employed. "Rich folks don't like it when their fancy plates fall and break," Glenda explained.

"So I quit school and got a job at Loose-Wiles in the bottoms. Momma still worked a little, so we were gettin' by." The somewhat good times didn't last long, though, Glenda explained, as her momma's condition worsened, forcing her to stop working altogether.

"We needed a little more money." Glenda hesitated, embarrassed. "I started seeing men for money, and that's how I got Bobby Joe." She smiled. "He's everything in the world to me."

Lulu cleared her throat. "Uh, Glenda, tell me if I'm asking you to tell tales out of school, but who is Bobby Joe's father?"

"Oh, I promised I'd never say," Glenda answered without hesitation. "He's a good man. He gives us a little money each month. It helps a lot."

Lulu figured she'd treaded as far as she should, and changed the subject to the future, dazzling Glenda with her lifelong dream of bright lights, adoring fans, fame and riches.

Glenda was understandably a little more practical. She repeated what her momma said her daddy liked to say when times got tough in the holler: "Every moment I'm feelin' good is a moment I ain't feelin' bad. And feelin' hungry ain't bad if I'm feelin' it with my family."

Fighting tears of her own, Lulu got up and walked over to Glenda. "Oh, please give me a big hug."

## WESTIN HAWKINS, PART THREE

**S**everal years after the family unit's European vacation, Gabriel had graduated Harvard and returned to Kansas City, not at all interested in the conglomeration of businesses upon which the family fortune had been built, but headstrong like his father and anxious to make his own success. Independent, yes, but pragmatic, too, as he willingly accepted his father's offer of a stake in Johnson county real estate to jump-start his career.

Unlike Marie, Westin did his best not to ask, or suggest, or in some manner try to guide his son's budding career. If the boy needed help or advice, he knew how to ask. From all appearances, though, and from what he was always pleased to learn from Marie, from others around town, Gabriel was off to a good start, depression be damned.

The splashy new home Gabriel was building in the exclusive Mission Hills enclave was a jolt to his father, even more so when he and Marie secretly drove by early one evening after the builder's workers had called it a day and they laid eyes for the first time on the mostly complete home. "He's building a palace," Westin muttered. Marie simply smiled and encouraged him to lose the frown and be happy for their son.

So, Westin was taken aback when Gabriel showed up unannounced at the sand and gravel office, awkwardly asking about his father's connections with Kansas City's underworld figures. Westin rarely discussed his mobster connections, and never with his son. Marie knew bits and scraps, but nothing of substance. But Gabriel wasn't raised on a desert island. His friends and classmates were the children of Kansas City's elites, the local business leaders, professionals and politicians, and the kids heard their parents' whispered rumors. Kids being kids, the rumors occasionally made their way to Gabriel.

"What kinda caper you got cookin' son?" Westin asked.

Gabriel chose an evasive response. "I've got a good business opportunity, father."

Westin was close to exploding, wanting to reach across the desk and slap his son's smug face. "Son, if you follow but one piece of advice I give you, let this be it: do not ever do business with those people. Ever!"

Gabriel didn't respond, dumbstruck by his father's anger.

"Now," Westin said dismissively with a wave of his hand, "be off and let us never speak of this again."

A year later came the late-night frantic call from Gabriel pleading for his father's immediate help finding the stolen car. Westin tried to talk his scared son off the ledge, ignorant of the big picture. Relenting, Westin assured Gabriel he'd make a call, wake someone up. Father and son spoke again the next day, Westin promising the police investigation would be kept under wraps and be handled by the department's top investigator.

Then, less than two days later, Marie, staying for several days at their son's home, fended off the bizarre attempted home invasion by a well-dressed man and came awfully close to blowing away the hot-in-pursuit Kansas City detective. Westin didn't know the details, but feared he knew the players. When he reached out to Tommy Lozarro, his old friend and now the family Don, and his call wasn't returned, Westin believed his worst fears confirmed.

Against this concerning backdrop Westin tossed and turned in bed, struggling to fall off to sleep. He heard the distant uneven tingling of the telephone in his downstairs study, followed by inaudible speaking, soft steps on the stairs, and light rapping on his bedroom door.

"Enter, Peter, I'm awake."

Westin's man servant, dressed in his bed clothes, opened the door and stepped into the bedroom. "You have an urgent call, sir?"

"My son? Marie?"

"No sir, the caller would not identify himself, except to say he is an old friend of yours, and that you would understand this."

"Thank you, Peter," Westin sighed. Throwing off the bedsheet, he swung his legs off the bed, stepped into his slippers and pulled on his robe. Westin hurried down the stairs in the low light and made his way into the study.

"This is Westin Hawkins," he said into the receiver. He listened to the voice on the other end of the call. "It must be close to midnight. This can't wait 'til morning?" Westin asked.

Westin listened, then responded, "Yes, I know Vince. Know of him, more than I know him. Who's the other?"

Westin listened. "Chicago? Yes, I know the name."

The caller spoke again.

"Okay, I'll get dressed and be there within the hour."

Westin hung up the receiver and considered his options. He picked up the receiver and dialed a number. "I'm sorry to wake you."

Forty minutes later, a hurriedly dressed Westin drove down the 12th Street viaduct into the deserted streets of the West Bottoms. Arriving at the closed gate to Hawkins Sand and Gravel yard he stepped out of his idling car and unlocked the heavy padlock as his night watchman, not long removed from living homeless in a lean-to shack of lumber scraps along the river on the edge of the company's property, limped slowly across the yard from the office building.

"Mr. Hawkins, sir?" the surprised, aging night watchman asked.

"Good evening, Thomas," Hawkins said, ignoring the strong odor of alcohol. "Open the gate and remain here. I'm expecting visitors shortly."

Hawkins returned to his car and drove to the office building. Inside, he turned on lights, straightened up the paperwork on his desk, and used his handkerchief to wipe from the chairs opposite his desk the ever-present thin layer of dust.

Returning to the front of the office Hawkins shut off the light and sat on the edge of a desk, watching the business yard through open window blinds. He didn't wait long.

Two dark sedans, one following closely behind the other, slowed and stopped at the gate. Hawkins watched as his night watchman stepped back from the first car, waving it forward. The second car pulled forward and cut its headlights. Two shadowy figures exited the second car, approaching the night watchman.

Hawkins opened the office building door, turned on the front office lights and walked slowly back to his office. He'd just eased down into the chair behind his desk when he heard a pair of footsteps scraping across the concrete floor. "Back here," Westin said in a raised voice.

Westin stood as Vinny and Paul walked cautiously into his office, eyes darting about, making sure they were alone.

"Get to the point, Vinny," Westin said as he sat, motioning to the empty chairs across from him. "It's late."

"Whadda ya know about your boy's bonds?" Vinny asked, getting straight to the point.

Westin stared up at Vinny, aware his smaller, well-dressed associate from Chicago had unbuttoned his suitcoat and was shifting slowly from behind Vinny. Westin's pounding heart started to race. In that moment he recalled the long-ago uttered words of his old friend, a friendly warning of sorts which, at the time, he considered surprisingly cynical. "Loyalty within the family," his old friend had told him, "is a convenient, romantic fiction, pliable and amorphous."

"Ya got any of the bonds here?" Vinny asked.

Westin stared at Vinny, knowing his time had come. Hmm, Westin thought, what would the cowboy say? "Fuck yourself, Vinny."

Vinny whipped his revolver from its shoulder holster, aimed and fired a shot into the middle of Westin's chest, then stepped closer and pulled off another round, plugging Westin in the middle of his forehead. Death was immediate.

Paul and Vinny ignored Westin's lifeless body, head thrown back, slumped in his chair, maneuvering around it to swiftly rifle through the desk drawers and a small cabinet in the office corner.

"There's no bonds here, Vinny," Paul said after the brief search. "We need to move."

A block east on a dark street the night watchman limped slowly along, his pants pocket bulging with a fistful of loose cash. He paused when he heard the first muted "pop," followed a couple seconds later by a second "pop," followed by silence. The recently homeless man hobbled forward to an alley and disappeared.

# WEST BOTTOMS

# NANA'S STORY, PART FOUR

**S**aturday, July 7, 1934. Three days into their red-hot relationship the mercurial small-town Kansas kids had their first fight. A real doozy. No fists, but shouting and screaming so loud Jimmy Dale's neighbors could hear it.

"California? Hollywood? Are you nuts, Nance?" Jimmy yelled, his face flushed.

"My plan, and it's my money, too, Jimmy," the young redhead shrieked. "We're going to California. Let's leave. Today!"

Jimmy had other ideas. A home, kids, and a business of his own. No more taking orders from an old man who didn't know shit. Eventually, exhausted, they arrived at a compromise. It was Jimmy's idea. They'd disappear into Kansas City, but stay no more than a year.

"I'm going home. Pack your stuff," Nancy ordered.

An hour later a flustered Nancy was back. "The cops talked to momma," she said excitedly, barely inside the door, suitcases in hand.

Jimmy leapt to his feet. "When?"

"Couple hours ago. They were lookin' for me. Momma lied. Told 'em she didn't know. They asked her where I was the night we stole the money."

"Shit, Nance, that's not good."

Nancy shuddered. "I'm scared, Jimmy."

"Okay, okay, let me think a second." Jimmy stared at the floor. "Okay, you pack up the cash and I'll grab some clothes. You drive your truck. Follow me."

With Jimmy in the lead the couple high-tailed it out of Flint, sticking to the back roads until reaching a remote fishing lake. Jimmy left the rutted lane, driving through thigh-high pasture before coming to a stop on a rise near the lake dam.

"C'mon, Nance," Jimmy said, jumping out of the Dodge.

"What're we doin' Jimmy?"

"Someone must've seen my car."

It dawned on Nancy what Jimmy was planning to do. "What? You're not makin' sense."

Jimmy waved. "C'mon, c'mon, help me push. Coppers must be lookin' for my car."

"They came to momma's house, not yours!"

"Help me push, damnit!"

After watching in silence as Jimmy's white Dodge slowly disappeared into the lake's muddy water, the couple secured their skimpy belongings in the bed of Nancy's truck and headed to Kansas City. The sack full of cash sat on the floorboard between Nancy's feet. Jimmy drove.

Less than three hours later, Jimmy slowed as they approached Bonner Springs, a rough-and-tumble blue-collar town near Kansas City, pointing to a collection of rental cabins alongside the highway. "Looks pretty deserted, Nance. Let's hole up here."

After booking a cabin for the week, Jimmy left Nancy to unpack and drove into Bonner Springs for food, cigarettes and beer. He wasn't gone long, returning with a Kansas City Star, too.

"Make us some sandwiches, Nance. Bring me a beer, too. I'm gonna check the ads."

Hands on hips, Nancy spun around. "I'm not your servant, Buster. Get your own damn beer." She checked the sack. "You get my chewin' gum?"

"It's in there. Bring me a pack of those Camels, too. And some matches."

"Grrr."

A few minutes later Jimmy whooped, then shouted for Nancy to come quick. "Lookee here, Nance, a market in Kansas City for sale. On the Missouri side. Coppers can't touch us there."

Nancy picked up the newspaper, squinting to read the print. "They want ten grand, Jimmy. We don't have it. We've got just over five."

Jimmy smiled. "You ain't seen Jimmy Dale Cooper negotiate, Nance. I'll get him down."

"Jimmy! You're a kid, goddamnit. You work at a lumberyard. Where'd you learn to negotiate?" Nancy threw down the newspaper and stomped away.

Jimmy jutted out his chin. "Nance, you're lookin' at the best haggler in Shawnee County."

"Jesus Christ," Nancy muttered.

Jimmy folded up the newspaper and stepped toward the door. "I'll be back, Nance. I'm gettin' us a market." He stopped and looked back, a big grin on his face. "Keep it on the sunny side, Nance."

"Stop sayin' that, Jimmy!"

A couple hours later, shadows long, Nancy heard the familiar rumble of her truck outside the cabin. She hurried to the window. Jimmy sat at the wheel for a moment, then got out, looking grim. Nancy returned to her chair as Jimmy came in and plopped down.

"The old fucker barely budged, Nance. He'll do $8,500, but he wants it by Sunday evening, tomorrow night."

"Well, we can still leave for California in the morning," Nancy said, smiling. "Maybe see the Grand Canyon along the way. I've always wanted to see it."

Jimmy wasn't listening. "Nance, this place is perfect. Right on a corner. Plenty of inventory in the back. People going in and out. Prob'ly worth more than ten grand. We gotta get it."

Jimmy stood up, head down, pacing in a tight circle.

Nancy watched for a moment. "What the fuck you doin'?"

"Shut up, Nance. I'm thinkin'. This helps me think."

A moment later he stopped, eyes wide. "Wait, wait. That first night we met, you told me about your aunt in Nebraska. Works at the train station."

"My cousin."

"Whatever." Jimmy stared at the floor for a moment. "Okay, the train comes in every Sunday morning, drops off cash for the banks. It sits in a safe 'til Monday morning." He turned and looked at Nancy. "That right?"

Nancy cleared her throat. "Let's just slow things down a bit, Cowboy." She rose from her chair. "Anna Mae and me were just doin' our best Bonnie Parker schemin'. Robbin' a train station wasn't ever a serious plan. We were just funnin' around." She added. "Jimmy, they got a shotgun under the counter."

Jimmy stepped over and held Nancy's shoulders, waiting until she looked up and their eyes met. "You trust me, Nancy Gleason?"

"Yes," she answered, tentatively.

"You love me?"

Nancy hesitated. "Do you love me?"

Jimmy grinned. "You know I do."

Nancy forced a smile. Jimmy pulled her in for a big hug. "We can do this, Nance. We just need a getaway car." He stepped back and turned toward the door.

"Wait, Jimmy, where you goin' now?"

"I got some more shoppin' to do." And lickety-split, Jimmy was out the door, the old blue Chevy's engine straining as he pushed it toward town.

"Nana?"

"Yes, dear."

"Where'd you learn the way you talk? You know, the 'hold your horses, buster.' Stuff like that. From your mother?"

"Cowboy."

"What, Nana?"

"It's 'hold your horses, cowboy,' not 'buster.'"

"Oh."

Foxy thought for a moment about Megan's question. "Well, yes, from my momma. I suppose it was after I learned my daddy didn't die in the great war. From time-to-time momma would throw one of those out, pretending like she was my daddy. You know, using a gruff voice like a man."

"So, this was the way your father talked. The one you never knew?"

"Yes."

"Hmm, interesting."

Foxy smiled. "Hey, Dr. Freud, don't be a smartass. Now, where were we?"

"Robbing the train station."

"Oh yeah. Well, I didn't wanna do it. Just knew it was a mistake, but we pulled it off."

Foxy continued her tale of that frenzied time. Jimmy returned to the cabin shortly after leaving with a pawn-shop pistol and maps of Kansas and Nebraska. The sun had set and it was getting dark quick. Jimmy shoved a fistful of cash into a pocket and the couple headed to Kansas City to find a getaway car.

Reaching Kansas City, Kansas, Jimmy cruised slowly down Minnesota Avenue pointing out two or three bars doing good business on a hot Saturday night, numerous cars parked along the curb.

"We got to the end of the main drag and had a nice view down into the bottoms. Jimmy turned down a street so we could circle back toward the bars he'd seen, thinkin' there had to be a car we could steal, but on this dark side street Jimmy spies a bar a couple blocks down. Not near the traffic as middle of town, so we drove down and checked it out."

Foxy described the plan: Jimmy goes inside, buys a couple beers, rushes back out if he sees anyone headed for the door. In the meantime, Nancy was to check out cars parked in the postage stamp parking lot next to the bar, looking for a key in the ignition switch. Decent cars only. It was bingo with the first car Nancy checked: a pretty Model A, key in the ignition.

Nancy turned and walked quickly to the bar's front door, stepping inside to see Jimmy getting chummy with a hot redhead at the bar, laying it on thick. Fortunately, Jimmy looked Nancy's way and she gave him the nod, then spun around and left, waiting for Jimmy on the sidewalk.

Foxy smiled wryly. "Cupcake, we're getting' ready to steal a car, rob a train station, and Jimmy's hittin' on a woman. Men!"

They both laughed.

Foxy continued. "So, he comes out and I tell him it's the gray Model A. He heads for it, and I head for the truck down the street a bit. Next thing you know I'm followin' Jimmy back to Bonner Springs."

An hour later the couple was packed and headed toward Falls City, Nebraska via Leavenworth and Atchison. The sun was just starting to peek over the horizon when Jimmy parked the stolen Ford along the curb at the edge of the sleepy town, two blocks from the train station.

"We got there an hour before the train was set to arrive. Anna Mae had told me it was pretty much always on time, though the amount of cash it dropped off could vary wildly. Jimmy lit up, so I said, "gimme one of those Camels.' Foxy laughed. "I told him I might as well be smokin' too."

"That's when it started?" Megan asked.

"Yup."

An hour later, right on time, the Missouri Pacific locomotive chugged slowly toward the station. Jimmy hopped out of the car and walked briskly down the deserted street. His timing was perfect. The train was just inching away from the station as Jimmy pulled the bandana over his nose, walked through the small station's door, through the tiny waiting area, and directly to the baggage room off the platform. Pulling his revolver as he entered the room, surprising the station manager, baggage handler, and the young woman Jimmy assumed to be Anna Mae, Jimmy seized the canvas cash bag before it could be locked away, turned and bolted for the door.

Sprinting all the way back to the car, gun in one hand, bag in the other, Jimmy tossed both on the floor board as he slid behind the wheel. He fired up the Ford and floored it, speeding out of town, travelling first toward Omaha, then east, then racing south to the Kansas border a short distance away. From there the couple continued on back roads all the way back to their cabin at Bonner Springs.

Safely back in the cabin, the exhilaration of actually pulling off an armed robbery finally kicked in as Nancy emptied the bag of cash on the floor. Fifteen bundles tumbled out. Jimmy dropped to the floor and started tallying their haul.

"Each bundle was a mix of denominations." Foxy explained. "Exactly $1,000 in each bundle. Fifteen bundles. Jimmy screams 'we did it, we did it, we're rich' so loud I just knew someone in one of the other cabins was going to hear it."

"So, $15,000 would buy you maybe a really nice house?" Megan asked.

"And a couple new cars." Foxy squished out her Camel, then fired up another. "While Jimmy was rolling on the floor in loose bills, reveling in what we'd done, I had a gnawing concern. So I asked him if he'd used his catchphrase when he – "

"Oh, the 'keep it on the top side' thing?"

"'Sunny side,' Sweetie, it's 'keep it on the sunny side.'" Foxy cleared her throat. "Well, he stopped the rolling around and thought for a second, then smiled and said 'yeah.' Dear, I could've strangled him. He said 'Nance, it's how people know me.' I counted to five, kept my cool, though I was steaming mad inside, then told him 'Jimmy, we don't want people to know who you are. Now count out your $8,500 and go buy us a market.'"

## WEST BOTTOMS

Foxy signaled for another drink.

"Oh yeah, I told him to steal us a Missouri license plate for the car, too. Next day, we drove into Kansas City early. I dropped Jimmy off at the market and drove over to a shop that painted the car red. Seriously, Babe, we both thought we'd pulled it off. Easy-peasy."

## WEDNESDAY, JULY 11, 1934, MORNING

Diehl flipped on the squad room lights, surprised to see the shades drawn and lights on in Capt. Mulroney's office. He'd no sooner sat down at his desk than Mulroney opened his door. "Diehl, need you now!"

Diehl grabbed his notepad and joined the Captain.

"Shut the door," Mulroney said as he drained his coffee before lighting a half-smoked cigar. "Some big shit's going down, Diehl. Got a call at home from Captain Stevens in Mission Hills. Two o'clock this morning a couple gangsters, Missouri side boys, were gunned down overnight at the Hawkins kid's home." Mulroney paused and re-lit the cigar, puffing until the end glowed red. He continued. "Apparently, they busted in and someone shot one in the gut, point blank, and nailed the other in the back as he tried to high-tail it outta the home."

"How do we know these guys are gangsters from Missouri?"

"The second guy, the one shot in the back, he made it out to their car. They found him slumped over the wheel."

"Where's the car registered?"

"Northland Salvage Company."

"So, a couple of old man Lozarro's boys," Diehl chimed in.

"Sure looks like it, Diehl." Mulroney gave up on the cigar and dropped it in his ashtray. "So, whadda ya got for me? Anything new?"

Diehl flipped open his notepad. "I'll get this typed up later. It was a long night."

Mulroney signaled Diehl to spit it out, so the young detective gave a summary of what he'd been told by Glenda, ending with his extraction of the family from Augie's bar.

"Where'd you stash the dame, Diehl?"

"I'm keepin' her safe, Cap."

Mulroney considered pushing for more detail but decided against it. "Very good, Diehl, get your report typed up. Keep me apprised. Just me, just the two of us."

"Mum's the word, Cap."

As Diehl stood to leave there was a large rap on the office door. Before Mulroney could respond, a uniformed sergeant opened the door. "Sorry, Cap, old man Hawkins is dead," he said excitedly. "Shot in the head."

"Suicide?" Mulroney asked.

"Not likely, Cap. One to the chest, one to the middle of his forehead."

"Where'd they find him?" Diehl asked.

"Hawkins Sand and Gravel down in the West Bottoms," the sergeant answered. "In his office, slumped over in his chair."

"Thank you, William," Mulroney said as the sergeant backed out, closing the door behind him.

"You believe in coincidences, Diehl?"

"I'm a step ahead of you, Cap. Seems they're rolling up anyone involved, or remotely involved in whatever's going on."

Diehl thought about the fearless little woman with a European accent. He was pretty certain she had no connection to whatever scheme Hawkins, his daddy, or both, were involved in, but she'd confronted a couple of likely gangsters. She'd seen 'em.

Diehl pushed his train of thought a little farther. Bad guys killed overnight at Hawkins' home. They already had the Hawkins kid, so they weren't looking for him. They were gunning for her, most likely. Damn, this must be pretty big to try rubbing out the kid's maid. Damn!

Diehl headed back to his desk, pausing to quickly scribble down his thoughts before pieces frittered away. Finished, he hustled across the squad room and soon was on his way to the West Bottoms and old man Hawkins' sand and gravel business.

Lulu tiptoed into her bedroom, careful not to startle the slumbering family scrunched together on her small bed. Gently, she poked Glenda on the shoulder. "Glenda, Glenda," Lulu whispered.

Glenda's eyes opened. With one arm wrapped around Bobby Joe, she turned toward Lulu.

"Glenda, I'm headed to work. Gotta scoot so I don't miss the trolley." Lulu glanced at her delicate watch. "There's food in the kitchen, but I'll stop by the market for more after work. My work number's by the telephone. Mark, Detective Diehl's, too." She added, firmly, "Remember, no one outside, don't answer the door. Stay safe."

Glenda smiled and mouthed "Thank you."

Diehl drove slowly into the shop yard at Hawkins Sand and Gravel, avoiding concerned workers clustered together. He parked alongside a department cruiser, waving off a local reporter on his way to the brick building from which the old man had overseen his sprawling business empire, created over several decades through innate guile, long hours, shrewd negotiating, kickbacks, greased palms.

"Hey, Diehl," Detective Reilly said from inside a cramped, tidy office, dominated by a desk, desk chair, and two chairs for visitors. Reilly reported Hawkins was found at daybreak by a worker looking for a cup of joe. "Doc's got the body," Reilly said, checking his notes. "Thinks they whacked him around midnight. He was sittin' in his chair. One to the forehead, one to the chest. Small caliber. No shells. Drawers opened," Reilly said, pointing toward a file cabinet and the desk. "Likely lookin' for something. No idea if they found it."

"Leads?" Diehl asked, swatting away a persistent fly. "Suspects?"

"Not yet," Reilly answered as he rifled through a small stack of papers on the desk. "He lives in a nice place up on Quality Hill and ran everything out of this dusty little shithole."

Diehl ignored the comment. "Killer take his wallet?"

Reilly picked up a brown cowhide wallet from the desk and handed it to Diehl, who thumbed through it and looked up at Reilly. "Must be a thousand bucks here, Reilly. You get this off the body?"

"Yes."

"What's that tell ya, Reilly?"

"Not a robbery. They left his sweat rag," Reilly chuckled, pointing to a knotted blue and white polka dot handkerchief looped over a nail tacked into the office wall below a sheathed Bowie knife resting on several nails also tacked into the wall. "Someone wanted him dead."

Diehl stepped behind the desk and studied close-up the dust-covered handkerchief, then the Bowie knife and its brittle, cow-hide leather sheath. "Hmm, you got any idea what these are, Reilly?" Diehl asked, pointing to the mementoes, stepping back from behind the dead man's desk.

"Nope."

Of course you don't, Diehl thought. "They got a night guard here. There's a gate off the road."

"Actually, they do, but he'd left for a couple hours to down a few at a place down the road. Wasn't here when the old man was killed. He's pretty shook, but didn't see anything."

"That normal, Reilly? Normal to leave for a couple of hours, at midnight, to go get tanked? At the time his boss gets whacked? Kinda convenient, don't you think, Reilly?"

"Umm . . . ."

Diehl wanted to explode. He took a deep breath. "Take the rummy downtown. Search him for a wad of bills. Throw him in the cooler, let him dry out if he needs it. Track down and talk to the barkeep and customers who might've seen him. Get a report on my desk before end of the day. I'll start sweating him later. Not you."

Reilly dropped the stack of papers on the desk. "Hold on, Diehl, this one's mine."

"No, it's not. Take it up with Cap, Reilly. No time to argue with you. I gotta check something across town."

Diehl eased his way out of the office. Outside, he walked past the handful of uniformed officers performing crowd control of the workers and local press, and the curious arriving in twos and threes to the morbid scene. It wasn't every day, after all, one of Kansas City's elites was gunned down in cold blood.

Diehl pulled out of the shop yard and headed south, weaving his way out of the West Bottoms. He hadn't gone far when a sudden fear for Augie struck him like a thunderbolt. Shit, he thought, I should've gone there first. Diehl cut a U-turn in the middle of the road and gunned the Studebaker as he raced back through the West Bottoms, across the Kansas River and up to Strawberry Hill on the Kansas side. He skidded to a stop in front of Augie's clapboard house next to the River City.

Pulling his revolver, Diehl moved quickly to the front door, which stood slightly ajar. He drew back the gun's hammer and kicked open the door. Arms outstretched he swung back and forth as he crept slowly inside the shadowy living room. He paused, listening. From the back of the home came a faint groan and what sounded like someone gasping for breath. Diehl moved slowly along the narrow hallway, floorboards creaking with each careful step.

A door at the end of the hallway was partially open. Diehl heard the unmistakable click of a gun's hammer being cocked. "Augie," Diehl yelled. No response. "Augie, this is Detective Diehl."

A strained "I'm here" came from the room.

"I'm coming in, Augie. Don't shoot me." Diehl said, lowering his weapon as he gently pushed the door open. The bedroom looked as if it'd been hit by a Kansas twister. Beaten and half-naked, Augie was on the other side of the bed, sitting on the floor, his back against a wall, left arm resting atop a turned over nightstand, his right hand gripping a single-shot .20-gauge shotgun laid across his lap.

Diehl hurried across the room and knelt next to the tough bar owner. Pulling a folded white handkerchief, Diehl daubed at the blood trickling down from a nasty gash above an eye swollen shut from what clearly was a severe beating.

"Two of 'em, Diehl," Augie struggled to say. "Glenda. Where'd she go? I wouldn't tell 'em." Painfully, he shifted slightly. "You just missed 'em. Thought they were comin' back."

"Brass knuckles?"

Augie nodded. "They busted some ribs, too."

"Seen 'em before, Augie?"

"Nah. Italians. Two big guys. Definitely muscle."

Diehl looked around the room. "Where's your phone, Augie?"

"Kitchen."

"Okay, stay put. I'll call in some uniforms and an ambulance." Diehl placed the calls then brought a wet dish towel back to the bedroom. Kneeling next to Augie, Diehl gingerly wiped drying blood from the struggling man's battered face. Several moments later there was a small clamor and sets of footsteps inside the front door.

"Back here," Diehl turned and shouted. He stood back and watched as Augie was carefully placed on a canvas stretcher, then followed the medics through the house and out to the ambulance. Turning to the uniformed officers, Diehl gave them instructions to protect the bar owner. Satisfied all was under control Diehl headed to the toney enclave of Mission Hills.

"Glenda, call my brother," Lulu urged with a hushed voice into the Macy's backroom telephone receiver. "Call him now."

"He's gonna be mad at me, Lulu."

"Call him, Glenda," Lulu said more firmly. "I'll do my best to come home early. Gotta go," Lulu said, hanging up the telephone and walking quickly back to the lady's lingerie department, forcing a polite smile at the well-heeled ladies she served with an expected deference understood by all.

"Hey, Diehl, your girlfriend called again."

"Give it a break, Brandt," a haggard Diehl said, easing into his desk chair and rolling a blank report form into his Underwood.

He'd learned in Mission Hills a couple hours after midnight two middle-age, armed males jimmied the back door of Gabriel Hawkins' stately home. No evidence of other entry, so they likely entered together. It was likely dark in the expansive kitchen into which the door leads, and the dead men likely didn't see the ambush that awaited them, inasmuch as the first shotgun blast came from very close range, blasting a jagged hole less than two inches across into the would-be assassin's gut, making mush out of his intestines. He dropped face first six feet inside the kitchen. Regrettably, the man's death would've been excruciating painful, and it wouldn't have been immediate.

As to the second ill-fated assailant, his unfired .38 snub-nose was found on the handmade terra cotta tile floor near the first man's body. He was found slumped over the steering wheel in the driver's seat of a Ford sedan parked along the street near the home's driveway. The blast that hit the second man likely came from the same gun and tore a hole four inches through his lower rear torso, at his waistline, representing a greater shot spread and a little further distance from the shooter than his dead partner. A sleepless neighbor reported "boom, boom" in fairly brief succession, maybe a second apart, indicating a violent event that climaxed quickly.

Hot, thick blood started pumping immediately from the second man's wound, the first evidence of it found a few steps outside of the home's back door. Within a few feet, and continuing down the drive to the car, blood was smeared in an almost unbroken, jagged line as the dying man first hobbled toward safety, before using everything he could to drag behind him an unresponsive right leg. The local doc who was awakened to view the bodies, pronounce death and offer an opinion as to cause, expressed initial surprise at the paucity of pooled blood on the Ford's car seat, making an informed guess death occurred within seconds of the man willing himself into the car. This thought was buttressed by how the body was found with the left leg hanging out the car, the door ajar.

The affluent, quiet community of Mission Hills marketed itself as a safe haven from Kansas City's daily criminality. The Kansas City Star's crime statistics and dramatic front-page headlines fueled sales even in the worst of times. Thus, the tax-conscious residents of Mission Hills employed a relatively skeleton law enforcement force, the main purpose of which was to run off questionable-looking characters, give stern warnings to the hot-rodding teenage scions and make sure, above all else, the negro help were beyond the city's limits by sundown.

To record the gruesome crime scene, the local newspaper publisher was roused from a deep sleep and directed to send his best photographer over to the Hawkins home. The groggy publisher plodded upstairs and awakened his twenty-year-old daughter, an aspiring novelist. The thrilled young woman bounded from her bed, dressed hurriedly, grabbed her go-bag of film, bulbs and her cherished Graflex Speed Graphic. Within a matter of minutes, she was on her way to the grisly crime scene, where almost certainly she set a new world record for total number of crime scene photographs.

A mystery, at least to the local officers investigating the shootings, was who did the shooting? And where is the gun? The logical working assumption was Gabriel Hawkins, the rich kid homeowner, shot the intruders, then, alarmed over what he'd done, fled in fear. Without wanting to reveal a more complete picture just yet, Diehl shared an educated hunch, informed by his recent experience at the home, something they might add to the mix. Needless to say, Diehl was pretty sure he knew exactly who'd taken down the bad guys.

Brandt finished off a day-old pastry and washed it down with lukewarm coffee. Standing, he brushed away crumbs and wandered slowly over to Diehl's desk, where the younger detective feverishly pecked away, intent on recording every detail, including those often considered insignificant by his peers, and even his own captain.

"Writing another book, Diehl?"

"You too, Brandt?" Diehl shot back without looking up from his typewriter.

"Your girlfriend called again. Not your sister, your girlfriend."

Diehl continued typing. "I don't have time for your nonsense, Brandt."

Brandt wasn't letting it go. "You know, Diehl, the one with that sweet southern drawl, leaves little cryptic messages?"

Diehl stopped and looked at Brandt. "Go on."

"She said the rube owns a corner market on the Missouri side."

"And?"

"That's it. An exact quote. Nothing more. 'Click,' she hangs up." Brandt shot a glance at Diehl's detailed report. "Guess she figures you'll understand. You understand her message, Diehl?"

Diehl ignored Brandt's prying question. He grabbed his telephone, shushing Brandt away. Waiting until the out-of-town flatfoot was definitely returning to his side of the squad room, Diehl dialed Lulu's home telephone number. He listened for one ring, then hung up the receiver. He dialed again. Same thing; one ring and he hung up. He dialed a third time. On the third ring the call was connected, followed by silence. "Jayhawk," he said.

"Detective Diehl?" asked a quiet voice.

Diehl cupped a hand over the receiver. "Glenda?" he asked softly. "You okay?"

"Yes, yes, we're fine," Glenda assured him. "Now, I know you're gonna be real mad at me, but I know where you can find the boy who stole Mr. Hawkins' car." She added, "It's just the weirdest thing."

Glenda quickly described how she struggled about whether to call her best friend, fearful Betty Jean would fret over her unexpected absence from work at their day job. Turns out, Betty Jean was worried, but then excited to share how she saw the car thief working behind the counter at Simpson's Market, Broadway and Southwest boulevards.

According to Betty Jean the fast-talking hick was bragging about low-balling the down-on-his-luck longtime owner, elderly Paul Simpson, in a cash on the table fire sale the day before, receiving a bill of sale, keys, landlord and utilities information. He and his wife were still getting their bearings.

"Wife?" Diehl asked.

"Well, Betty Jean said she didn't see a ring on the woman's finger," Glenda said. Laughing, she added, "Betty Jean said the wife wears her makeup a tad heavy."

"Good to know," Diehl said, jotting another note.

"What about the car, Glenda?"

"She didn't say anything about it, Detective Diehl."

Diehl quickly considered his options. "You got some sunglasses, Glenda?"

"Not here."

"I'm sure Lulu does. Scrounge around and find a pair. I'll be there in thirty minutes."

Diehl stood, looked across the squad room. "Brandt," he shouted. "Need you, now. Let's go."

Brandt grabbed his suitcoat off the back of his chair, meeting Diehl at the squad room door. The two men hustled down the stairs in silence, exiting the building into the blast furnace heat of yet another in a string of unremittingly brutal Kansas summer days.

"What's up, Diehl?" Brandt asked as they settled into Diehl's Studebaker.

"You know about my car theft case?" Diehl asked, shooting a glance at Brandt to gauge his reaction.

"A bit?"

"How much you know?"

"Enough, but never enough, right Diehl?"

# WEST BOTTOMS

# WEDNESDAY, JULY 11, 1934, MIDDAY

Twenty minutes after leaving downtown, Diehl and Brandt pulled into Lulu's Rosedale neighborhood of tightly packed homes. Glenda, wearing a flowery dress borrowed from Lulu's closet, hurried out the front door toward the street. She skidded to a stop as Brandt eased his beefy body from the passenger seat and squeezed into the back seat.

Diehl leaned over and motioned Glenda into the car. "It's okay. He's okay."

Glenda's door was closing as Diehl accelerated forward. "Your sunglasses are very fashionable," he said, attempting to ease the tension he knew Glenda was feeling.

"Your sister's got very nice things, very nice clothes."

"Macy's discount."

Within a few moments the group was traveling east on Southwest Boulevard.

"State line," Brandt said matter-of-factly as they crossed State Line Road.

A few blocks further east the traffic picked up as they reached a neighborhood of two-story walk-ups and small commercial buildings. Glenda pointed ahead to Simpson's Market. Diehl cruised by slowly, then circled most of the block, parking on a side street with a view of the market's backside.

"See that shiny red Ford, Brandt?" Diehl asked.

"Yup," Brandt responded. "Color of the stolen car?"

"Fancy green. More gray than green."

Diehl turned to Glenda. He handed her a $5 bill. "You shop. I'll be your man. If it's the kid from the River City give me a sign, tell me 'Mom's coming to town,' or something like that. Something about 'mom.'"

"Got it."

Diehl and Glenda crossed the street diagonally toward the front of the market. Brandt headed straight to the alley and the shiny red Ford parked near the market's rear door. Diehl reached the market's front door first, opening it for Glenda. An otherwise attractive young woman wearing a bit too much rouge, a bit too much mascara, a bit too much eye shadow, and ruby red lipstick sat perched on a stool behind the store's crowded counter flipping through a recent edition of True Story magazine, her mouth rhythmically opening and closing as she chomped on a bit too many sticks of gum.

"Can I help?" Nancy Gleason asked, looking up from her magazine.

"Thanks, just need to pick up a few things," Glenda said over her shoulder as she turned down the market's narrow aisle, her eyes scanning the scant offering of canned goods. Diehl moseyed along the wall shelves, pretending to show interest in a tin of saltines. No sooner had he placed it back on the shelf than a swinging door leading to the back flew open and, like a manic whirling dervish, Jimmy Dale Cooper flew into the market's public area, several cases of cigarettes stacked one atop the other, wedged under his chin.

"Found 'em, Nance," he said triumphantly. Jimmy squatted down, dropping the boxes to the floor, oblivious of his two customers.

"Dear," Glenda said over the top of the aisle shelves, holding up a can in each hand, "Momma might like some tomato soup and corned beef."

Diehl nodded and the two walked toward the counter.

Meanwhile, in the alley behind the market, Brandt ambled past the Ford, slowing to peek inside at the car's messy, dust-covered interior. After passing the car Brandt continued a short distance, slyly scanning for curious onlookers. Returning to the Ford Brandt pulled out his pocket knife and knelt down between the car and the market's back wall.

After glancing up and down the alley Brandt gently scraped a barely noticeable area of red paint near the bottom of the rear wheel well. The rubbery red overcoat easily peeled away, revealing a greyish-green undercoat. Satisfied the detectives had the car they were seeking, Brandt rose and walked nonchalantly back to Diehl's car, pausing only to memorize the Ford's stolen Missouri license plate.

No sooner had Brandt crossed the street, than Diehl and Glenda came around the corner, a small paper sack in hand. Without a word the three were quickly back in the car.

"Glenda made our boy," Diehl said over his shoulder as he turned west on Southwest Boulevard, retracing the route to Lulu's Rosedale home.

"The Ford was painted very recently. Cheap job," Brandt reported. "Original coat is a light shade of green. Missouri plate, likely stolen." Brandt cleared his throat. "We've got enough to grab him, Diehl, but, I'm thinkin' we may wanna spin this a little different, if you're game."

Diehl turned to Glenda as they slowed, turning onto Lulu's street. He fished a paper napkin from his shirt pocket. Showing it to Glenda, he asked, "This is the number where the gangster can be reached? The guy who nabbed Hawkins?"

"Yes, he told me to ask for Vinny," Glenda answered nervously as Diehl parked along the curb. "Whatcha got in mind, Detective Diehl?"

Diehl thought before answering. "I'm not sure, Glenda," he said, honestly. "Stay by the phone. I may need you to make a call later on." He nodded toward the house. "You scoot on up there and stay inside. No more calls. Stay inside."

Diehl watched Glenda safely inside the home as Brandt returned to the front seat. Brandt spoke first as they made their way out of Lulu's neighborhood. "There a place nearby where we can grab a sandwich and soda?" he asked. "Two heads are better than one, Diehl, and I've got an idea or two."

"Yes, two heads are better than one. I know a place."

Paul and Vinny shared a table in a back corner of the smoke-filled Tallman's Grill. Vinny tore off another hunk of bread, jamming it into his mouth before washing it down with a gulp of red wine.

The noon-day crowd had thinned, leaving a collection of mobsters and those who operated around the edges of organized crime, the family's useful idiots and wannabes. The grill's front door opened, early afternoon light streaming in, back-lighting two uniformed Kansas City, Missouri officers who stepped in, pausing just inside as they read the room.

Conversation and laughter in the grill dropped to a murmur as the lead flatfoot, a stout, older officer, marched to the back of the room while his younger partner remained posted near the door.

Vinny set his wine goblet on the table and wiped his mouth as the older officer eased past an empty table and walked to Vinny's side, the officer's back to the room.

"Good afternoon, Officer O'Donnell," Vinny said, not bothering to look up. He pulled a thick envelope from his breast pocket, placed it on the table and slid it toward O'Donnell, who picked it up, holding it close to his mid-section as he thumbed the stack of bills.

Satisfied, O'Donnell jammed the envelope in his front pants pocket. "Where are they?" he asked.

Vinny nodded toward two middle-aged men sitting quietly at a nearby table. "Charlie and Tony."

"They armed?"

"They're clean, Officer O'Donnell," Vinny answered. "Be nice to my boys."

O'Donnell grunted as he turned and summoned his partner. "Jones!" he shouted.

Paul watched with interest as the staged drama played out in front of him. Charlie and Tony were frisked, cuffed and led to a waiting patrol car. A moment later the car's wailing siren announced its departure for the cow town's police HQ where the two veteran hoodlums would be paraded for the insatiable local press, separated, interrogated and, sometime in the wee hours after the annoying newshounds had finished the next morning's sensationalized reporting on the quick arrests in the gangland slaying of business magnate Westin Hawkins, the two would be ushered to the sidewalk and released without charge.

"They'll be here for lunch tomorrow," Vinny said. "Heat's on. Kansas coppers are pushing hard."

"What happened at the house, Vinny?"

Vinny took another drink of wine. "Fuck, Paul, that fuckin' big mouth Joey must've got sloppy. Got 'em both killed."

"Well, we're back at square one, Vinny. No car, no package, the whore knows too much."

"I've got someone working on it, Paul."

Paul pushed back from the table. "I'll be at the hotel, Vinny. Call me when you hear somethin'."

"I'll give you a ride."

"I'll walk."

The walk-ups and trees west of Simpson's Market were casting creeping shadows as Diehl parked his Studebaker across from the alley behind the market. The red Ford was where it had been several hours earlier.

"Sign on the door says they close in fifteen minutes," Diehl said as Brandt checked the ammo in his .38 revolver. "You take the back."

As Diehl crossed the street toward the market's front door, Brandt took a position between the red Ford and the solid back door. A tiny bell made a tinkling sound as Diehl opened the market door. A working-class woman studiously browsed a shelf along the back wall. Nancy, sitting on the stool behind the counter, looked up from her dime-store novel, recognizing Diehl. "Back for more, mister?"

"Yes, ma'am," Diehl said as he pulled out his badge. "You're under arrest."

Nancy stopped chomping on her wad of gum. Instinctively, she leapt off the stool, freezing in place as Diehl leveled his service revolver at her chest. "Down on your knees. Now!" Diehl ordered. Quick as a flash Nancy was frisked, in cuffs behind her back. Diehl pulled her up from the floor and pushed her down on the stool.

"Jimmy!" Nancy screamed. "Coppers!"

Diehl heard a ruckus in the back room. Seconds later Jimmy burst through the backroom door and slid to a stop almost face-to-face with the imposing detective's gun pointed at his chest. Jimmy's eyes darted back and forth between Diehl's gun in one hand, and his shiny copper badge in the other. Jimmy wheeled and bolted back through the swinging door. Dodging stacked boxes Jimmy raced to the alley door, exploding through it where his delicate facial features met Brandt's sledge-hammer fist. Jimmy flew back, crashing against the door, dropping to the ground as his knees buckled, blood gushing from his nose.

"Goddamnit, mother fuck," Jimmy squealed, "you broke my fuckin' nose!"

Brandt stepped forward, putting his full body weight into a violent punch down to the top of Jimmy's head. His brain totally scrambled, Jimmy crumpled face-first onto the alley's weathered bricks. Careful not to crush any bones, Brandt gently stepped onto Jimmy's fingers. No response. Brandt leaned down and rolled the limp body over and cuffed Jimmy's wrists behind his back. Brandt did a quick pat-down for weapons, then rolled him over and searched the front side, finding a small, pearl-handled revolver, Boy Scout pocket knife, and a car key. After dropping the car key and Jimmy's weapons into his jacket pocket, Brandt grabbed a handful of shirt with one hand, opened the door with the other, and dragged Jimmy's limp body inside the market's storeroom.

Diehl turned to the petrified shopper across the store and showed her his badge. "Police business, ma'am," he said calmly, nodding his head toward the front door. "Store's closed." The woman scurried toward the door, dropping her shopping basket along the way.

Diehl walked out from behind the counter and locked the market's front door, flipping around the open/closed board that hung in the window. As he turned back, a perspiring Brandt kicked open the storeroom's swinging door and dragged the unconscious Jimmy into the front, dropping him like a sack of potatoes next to the counter. Breathing heavy, Brandt pulled a wadded-up handkerchief from his pants pocket and wiped the sweat from his face and neck.

"You've killed him, you fuckin' brute!" Nancy shrieked.

Brandt looked at Diehl. "He ran into the door. He's fine."

"Wake him up," Diehl ordered. "Let's arrest him and get outta here."

Brandt leaned over and patted Jimmy's cheeks a few times. No response. Brandt looked around, grabbed a bottle of rubbing alcohol from a close-by shelf and dribbled a small stream across Jimmy's face. Like he'd stuck a licked finger in a light socket, Jimmy sprang back to life, squirming and grimacing on the store's checkered floor, followed by an uncontrollable stream of expletives. "Fuck, fuck, fuck, you fuckin' son of a bitch."

Brandt gave him a swift kick in the gut, doubling him up. "Shut up you whiney baby."

"Prop him up, Brandt."

Diehl leaned over and held his badge a few inches from Jimmy's face. "It's blurry," Jimmy said, blinking his eyes. "Wipe my eyes you fuckin' copper."

Diehl pulled out a handkerchief and wiped Jimmy's eyes. "Here, Jimmy, see it now?"

"Kansas!" Jimmy exclaimed. "It says Kansas. This is Missouri. I took it in Kansas, not - "

"Jimmy!" Nancy screamed. "Shut the fuck up!"

Diehl and Brandt looked at each other.

"She wasn't even there," Jimmy said. "Let her go."

"She was there for the armed robbery," Brandt said. "We're arresting you for both."

"But that was Nebraska, this is Missouri," Jimmy sputtered.

"Jimmy!" Nancy screamed. "Can you be any more stupid?"

Diehl stood and looked at Brandt. "I guess he can be," Brandt said.

"My God, Jimmy, just shut the fuck up for once in your life," an exasperated Nancy said. "Jesus Christ almighty."

Brandt grabbed Jimmy by the scruff of his neck and lifted him to his feet and, following Diehl and Nancy, led him out onto the sidewalk where the detectives were met by a gaggle of nosey neighbors. Jimmy and Nancy, their reality fully sinking in, were mute as each was stuffed into the Studebaker's back seat. Brandt jogged across the street into the alley and, in a moment, was backing the red Ford down the alley toward Diehl.

Brandt sped forward, Diehl close on his tail. Brandt took a fast right, driving a short distance before swerving onto a road headed due west past a mix of homes, vacant land and the random small business. The pervasive stench of tens of thousands of corralled livestock grew stronger as the two cars approached the West Bottoms stockyards.

Brandt turned north on Genessee, a main drag of the West Bottoms, slowing for the late day congestion. A couple blocks past the massive Livestock Exchange Building, the brick-and-mortar shrine to the riches generated by the plains' bounty, Brandt made a quick right onto a narrow street, slowing as he turned into the short drive of a non-descript brick warehouse. He stopped in front of a large garage door and tooted the Ford's horn. Immediately, the heavy wood door slid open and Brandt idled forward into the building's open, dim interior, followed closely by Diehl and their prisoners. The door slid shut with a heavy wham.

Diehl stopped behind the red Ford and killed the engine, astonished to see a handful of clean-cut men in suit pants and loosened ties gather around Brandt, joined by another, maybe a generation older than the rest. After a few seconds of conversation the group dispersed, save for the older gentlemen and two of the younger associates who approached Diehl's Studebaker. The older man led the way, smiling and offering his hand as Diehl stepped from his car.

"Detective Diehl, Special Agent Bob Morris, Division of Investigation," the federal agent said. "Nice to meet you. Let's make your passengers comfortable."

164

Diehl stepped back and watched as the two men roughly his age, followed by Morris, firmly hustled Jimmy and Nancy past a dark coupe and out of sight down a hallway at the building's back end. Diehl scanned the large garage. At least a half-dozen additional men were scattered about at makeshift work stations, otherwise occupied with typing, studying a large metropolitan area map, speaking on the telephone, quietly conversing. The place had all the appearance of an efficient, secret beehive of something important.

Brandt sauntered back. "Sorry, Diehl, had to pee really bad."

"So, this is the place you said we could use, the place where we'd hole up with the car?" Diehl asked.

"Yup."

"And you're a part of whatever this is?"

"Yup."

"Hold on, hold on, is your name even Brandt?"

"Actually, it is. That's my name," Brandt said, showing Diehl his DOI badge. "Special Agent Timothy Brandt, Division of Investigation."

"Well, I'll be damned," Diehl said, shaking his head. "Wait, is this how you knew about whatever happened in Nebraska, the robbery?"

"Uh huh. Wanted circular from Nebraska. Looked like it could be them, but didn't know for sure until Einstein confirmed it."

"What's going on here, Brandt?" Diehl asked, motioning to the hum of activity in the garage.

"It's a secret, Diehl," Brandt said, using his thumb and a finger to pinch his lips shut. "Mum's the word. You were never here." Brandt added, "Oh yeah, Cap can't know, your little sis can't know. Got it?"

"Mum's the word."

Brandt loosened his tie. "Let's grab a pastry and some coffee, then go talk to Miss Spitfire. I'm guessing she was along for the thrill of it. She'll let the cat outta the bag."

Sure enough, Diehl and Brandt had no more than removed Nancy's cuffs, sat down alone with her at a wobbly wood table in a makeshift interrogation room than it all came spilling out, starting with a blind date at a bowling alley in a dusty Kansas town. The armed robbery was the most exhilarating thing she'd ever done, and she was richer now than she could've ever dreamed. She didn't know anything special about Hawkins' car, and they'd found no treasures in it, though they hadn't thought to look. Diehl scribbled notes, catching up only when Nancy stopped to catch her breath. An hour later the two men stepped out of the room, leaving Nancy with a glass of water, ashtray, box of matches and a pack of Camels.

"Got a typewriter and paper, Brandt?" Diehl asked. "We can talk to Jimmy after I've got it all typed up, with Nancy's John Hancock."

"Sounds good. Follow me."

# WEDNESDAY, JULY 11, 1934, LATE AFTERNOON

Lulu walked quickly up the street from her trolley stop and turning the corner into her neighborhood, picked up the pace. Arriving at her front door she slowly knocked three times. Pausing a couple seconds Lulu repeated the all-safe signal. After more than a few seconds and no answer she tried again, a bit more forcefully. Again, no answer.

Concerned now, fearful of the scene she might find inside, Lulu quietly inserted a skeleton key in the front door's keyhole and, trying to be quiet as a church mouse, slowly turned the key, cautiously turned the door handle and gently pushed with her shoulder. The door didn't budge. She pushed a little harder, but it still didn't budge. Lulu was momentarily confused until realizing she'd just locked an unlocked door that should've been locked. Now she was really concerned.

Unlocking the door, Lulu gently pushed with her shoulder, opening it a crack. She leaned against the door frame and, balancing on one foot then the other, slipped off her emerald green Macy's discount heels. Pushing the door open a little more, Lulu peered inside, relieved not to see signs of a violent struggle. Lamps, furniture, plants were where she'd last seen them that morning.

Lulu slid inside and tiptoed forward a few feet. Nothing out of place in the living room, dining room, and what she could see of the kitchen down the home's only hallway. Lulu froze and listened, hearing only her elderly neighbor's yippy dog. She crept cautiously down the hallway, peering into each bedroom, the tiny bathroom and, finally, the kitchen. Satisfied she was alone, Lulu returned to the living room and dialed the telephone number she knew by heart. After a number of rings a gruff male voice answered.

"This is Detective O'Hanlon, Diehl's desk."

"Detective Diehl, please."

"He's not here, ma'am."

"Okay, when'll he be back? It's critical I speak to him as soon as possible."

Detective O'Hanlon chortled before answering. "I've no idea, ma'am. Wanna leave a message?"

"Yes, yes, uh, tell him the bird has flown the coop. He'll understand."

"And you are?" O'Hanlon asked.

Recalling her big brother's warning not to trust anyone, Lulu quickly hung up the receiver. Confused and stressed, unsure what to do now, Lulu walked out onto her front porch and sat down on the step, leaving the door open so she could hear the telephone ring. Staring straight ahead, elbows on her knees, chin resting snugly in her hands, she said to no one, "I picked a horrible time to stop smoking."

Diehl finished typing Nancy's long-winded confession and pulled the last page from the DOI's standard Royal typewriter. He leaned back and quickly perused the finished product. Satisfied every detail was included, no matter how seemingly inconsequential, he signaled to Brandt. "We just need her to read and sign it," Diehl said as Brandt ambled over. "Got some more cigs?"

"Let's go," Brandt said.

Ten minutes later, signed confession in hand, the two men strategized before paying a visit to Jimmy. "I'm thinkin' Jimmy's gonna be a harder nut to crack," Brandt offered. "My suggestion is we – "

"Hold on, Brandt, I've got a couple questions."

"Okay, Diehl, make it quick. We got work to do."

"Right, right. So, here's the deal, Brandt. Last night I stop at O'Grady's to grab a sandwich. Not the fanciest place, if you know what I mean. In walks Chief Finney and the missus, dressed to the nines, not there to eat. Clearly, they were headed somewhere else. Know what I mean?"

Brandt nodded.

"Well, Chief Finney shoos his wife away and pulls up a seat. Asks me about the Hawkins car case, then tells me a couple unrelated, really concerning things. Warnings. Very vague, nothing specific. Then he asks me about you. That caught me by surprise. He tells me two things: 'trust you, use you.' Whole thing lasts a couple minutes, and he leaves. Odd, huh?"

"Uh huh."

"So, Brandt, Chief Finney just happens to stumble across me eating at O'Grady's, tells me to reach out to you, trust you, and twenty-four hours later here we are, in this secret DOI operations center I'm pretty sure I wasn't supposed to know about. What's going on?"

"What's going on? I'm helpin' you bust a car theft," Brandt answered.

"No offense, Brandt, but we've busted the car theft. That's done. We got the car thief, we've got the car. This thing's bigger than a simple car theft. Has been from the start."

"Ya think?" Brandt responded dismissively. "Look, Diehl, we were hot on Hawkins' car. Two steps ahead of ya the whole time," Brandt explained matter-of-factly. "We would've found it first, but your whore - "

"Her name is Glenda."

"Glenda. Yes, Glenda, I'm sorry. So, Glenda blunders across the car and, well, plans changed. They evolved. Plans are always evolving. And here we are."

"You gonna tell me more?" Diehl asked, pretty sure he knew the answer.

"Nope."

"Okay, let's go talk to Jimmy," Diehl said.

"Hold on, Diehl. As I started to say, we need to deal with Jimmy a little different. He won't crumble like his moll. When we go in there, and no matter what I do or say, you be his friend. Ignore me. Don't stop being his friend, being nice to him. Got it?"

Diehl thought for a moment about Brandt's plan. "Okay, let's give it a go."

Diehl and Brandt found the cocky fast-talker pacing in a tight circle, wrists cuffed behind his back.

"Seen this before, Diehl?"

"In one form or another, too many times."

Diehl laid Nancy's three-page confession on a table in the middle of the room, along with an ashtray and box of matches. A burning bare light bulb hung from the room's tall ceiling. Jimmy slowed his pacing when he saw Brandt. The pacing stopped altogether when Brandt stripped off his suitcoat, locked the door and slowly rolled up his shirt sleeves, revealing oversized forearms.

"Jimmy, stop fidgeting, please, and sit down," Diehl asked politely.

Continuing to stare at Brandt's clenched fists, Jimmy lowered himself into a chair opposite Diehl, freezing as Brandt moved behind him, leaned over and unlocked the cuffs.

"Jimmy," Diehl started in a calm voice, "I think we got off on the wrong foot this - "

"Stop!" Jimmy interrupted, rubbing his uncuffed wrists. "I gotta know. It's driving me crazy, can't stop thinkin' about it. It was perfect. How'd you know, goddamnit?"

Diehl and Brandt looked at each other.

"How'd we know what, kid?" Diehl asked.

"How the fuck did you know about Nebraska?"

Diehl pointed at Brandt. "Tell him."

"We didn't, Jimmy. It was a hunch. You copped to it there at the market," Brandt said dismissively.

It took a few seconds, but then Jimmy remembered. "Oh shit."

"And your gal told us everything," Diehl added, sliding the signed confession across the table. "That's her signature, Jimmy. Recognize it?"

"Hmm, I dunno. Maybe."

Brandt decided to push a little harder. "You finish high school, Jimmy?"

"Course I did," Jimmy spat back. After a moment he angrily asked, "You callin' me stupid?"

Brandt lit a cigarette. "I rest my case."

Diehl tapped the table top lightly, regaining Jimmy's attention. He gathered up Nancy's confession and laid it off to the side. "Want a cigarette, Jimmy?" Diehl asked, shoving an unopened box across the table.

"Parliaments are for sissies."

"Jesus Christ," Brandt muttered. "This ain't gonna work, Diehl. Let's take this weasel downtown and hook him up with his new boyfriends." Brandt moved closer, anger rising. "You don't wanna help us out, Jimmy, don't wanna cut your prison time? I don't give a shit. Fine by me. Diehl here thinks we need you, but I don't. You'll come out a fuckin' old man, and that's just Kansas. Then we'll ship your sorry ass up to Nebraska and you'll do time up there. Fuckin' dumbass."

Diehl reached for the cigarettes. "Parliaments or nothin', Jimmy?"

"Hold on, hold on, let me think. Okay, gimme those matches. Maybe we can cut a deal?" Jimmy asked, regaining a hint of his swagger.

"Yeah, we've got an idea or two," Brandt responded, nodding at Diehl.

"Jimmy, you do it like we set it up and we ask the law in Nebraska to go easy on your gal. No jail time."

"They'll do that?"

"No guarantees, but we'll try," Diehl promised. "You do your part and we help you, too."

"No jail time for me?"

"Nah," Brandt said, "you're doin' time, but maybe less."

Over the next forty-five minutes Jimmy admitted to every line of Nancy's confession, even adding several unsolicited details. Then, Diehl and Brandt explained what Jimmy needed to do to gain their good word for less jail time, and maybe none for Nancy. "That's it?" Jimmy asked, surprised by the simplicity of the plan. "Is there a catch?"

"That's it, no catch," Brandt answered, checking his watch. "We do it in a few hours."

"I'm in."

"Good. Jimmy, I'm gonna type up one of these for you to sign," Diehl told him. "Same as what Nancy did."

"Okay."

At that moment there was a light rap at the door. Brandt unlocked and opened the door, and was handed a note. After shutting the door Brandt read the note as Diehl and Jimmy continued to talk. "Diehl," Brandt interrupted, holding up the note and nodding toward the door.

"Be right back, Jimmy."

Diehl followed Brandt out, shutting the door behind him. Brandt handed him the note. Looking confused after reading the note, Diehl handed it back.

"So, Brandt, how exactly do you know about Lulu's call? What she said, what O'Hanlon said?"

Brandt folded the note and slipped it into his shirt pocket. "Sounds important, Diehl. You better call your little sis."

Brandt led Diehl back into the garage area and a telephone at an empty desk. He stepped back as Diehl dialed Lulu's number. Brandt did his best to eavesdrop, but Diehl had his back turned, speaking in hushed tones. After some back and forth with his little sister Diehl hung up the receiver and looked at Brandt. "She's pretty frazzled. Actually, more scared than frazzled. Everyone's scared."

"So who calls to set up the meet?" Brandt asked. "You? Me? The professor?"

"Glenda's making the call."

"I thought she – "

Diehl interrupted. "Glenda's making the call."

"Okay, okay, the plan's still on," Brandt said, picking up a metal toolbox off a table. "Let's see what's so important about that Ford."

Dressed only in his boxer trunks, Paul was lounging on his hotel room bed reading the Kansas City Star when the telephone jingled. "Yes, put him through," he said to the hotel clerk.

"Paul?"

"Whadda ya got for me, Vinny?"

"I think we've found the car," Vinny said.

Perking up, Paul set the paper aside and swung his legs over the side of the bed. "Where?"

"Not where, but who," Vinny answered. "Your southern belle, the whore, she called the club, asking for you. Says she's got it, wants to cut a deal. I talked to her, Paul."

"A deal?"

"Yeah, three grand for the car. And," Vinny added, "we leave her, her kid, and her mom alone."

"That's it?"

"No, no, this dame of yours is really somethin'. Small bills, meet tonight at midnight on 16th in the West Bottoms, east of the exchange building, between Wyoming and Liberty. We drive in from the west. One car. Any hanky-panky, she says, and she bolts."

"Hmm, I dunno, Vinny. This smell okay to you?"

"Paul, Paul, I been tellin' you from the start I think the dame's got somethin' to do with this." Vinny pressed on. "She's all snuggly with Hawkins and everything. I think he was the mark, but now she's making lemonade out of a lemon. Know what I mean?"

Paul thought for a moment, a little uneasy with the fortuitous call, but not necessarily wanting to pass on getting his hands on the Ford. "Yeah, yeah, that might make sense."

"So, I've gotta couple boys down there now, checkin' out the area. I'll scrape together the cash and - "

"Whoa," Paul interrupted. "Just get a bunch of Washingtons and stuff 'em in a bag. We're not handin' over three grand."

"Gotcha."

"I need a bath and somethin' to eat. Pick me up in a couple hours?" Paul asked.

"Sure, Paul, we'll take a swing through the bottoms and come back for momma's pasta. Bring your gas mask," Vinny laughed before hanging up.

## WEDNESDAY, JULY 11, 1934, LATE EVENING

Dusk was turning to dark as Paul rode in silence while Vinny noted points of interest in the cramped Kansas City West Bottoms. He slowed and nodded down a side street. "That's where we meet. Tonight we turn here and pull up half a block. She'll be waiting there, facing us."

Paul studied the small business buildings framing the street. Though the July evening traffic on nearby Genessee was moderate, the two-block long 16th Street was a ghost town. Workers and managers had long left for home, and the massive rail yard immediately east was jam-packed with standing rail cars.

"Hawkins' dame works down here, Vinny?" Paul asked.

"Yeah, north a bit, over in the industrial area, but she didn't show up today. She knows the area. Picked a good spot over here near the stockyards."

The two mobsters spent the next fifteen minutes or so driving and discussing alternative routes out of the West Bottoms, and contingency plans. Vinny was quietly impressed with the young Chicagoan's unexpected thoroughness. All business, no fun and games with this kid, he thought.

For his part, Paul was struggling to rid himself of a concern he might be walking into a trap, one that in hindsight would be quite evident. But without more than an uneasy hunch he was reluctant to pass on the meet. He certainly didn't want to come across as weak-kneed or wishy-washy in front of the Kansas City boys. That would certainly get back to his father. Vinny's theory was, he had to admit, somewhat logical. The hooker pinches the rich boy's car, learns it's worth more than that just a heap of metal, attempts to shake down the rich boy, but he gets swooped up. Now, she's shaking down the men she knows are desperate to find the car. Yeah, it does make sense, he thought. His father would be decisive, and so would he.

"We're set, Vinny. Let's go eat."

A curious interest in Hawkins and his expensive Ford was clear to Diehl from early on in the investigation. Initially, it smelled like the garden-variety odor of a rich, connected daddy and strings being pulled downtown. Quickly, though, ruthless mobsters inexplicably joined the search, and now were seemingly rolling up whatever illegal scheme it was that connected them to Hawkins, his daddy, and maybe others unknown.

Finally, though, Diehl and Brandt likely had possession of their enigma's Rosetta Stone. They just had to find it. After a frustratingly fruitless search of the Ford's floorboards, trunk, seats, dashboard, engine well, it was Brandt who spied an innocuous small cloth tab protruding a fraction of an inch from the bottom edge of the passenger door panel. No more than a gentle tug with a pair of pliers and the panel popped loose, revealing a narrow compartment cradling an expensive leather satchel containing maybe a hundred crisp, never circulated Kansas development bonds.

The two men didn't know if the bonds were stolen, forged, or both, and at 10:00 p.m. they wouldn't be finding out this night, but it didn't matter: tens of thousands of dollars payable by the State of Kansas answered the question why there was such intense interest in Gabe Hawkins' fancy Ford.

Diehl checked his watch. "Let's put it all back together. Time's gettin' short." Diehl held up the stack of bonds. "These too, ya think?"

"Absolutely," Brandt answered without hesitation. "The bad guys need to find 'em." He didn't add his strong hunch their lamb on a stake, Jimmy, had little chance leaving the scene with a beating heart, and even less if the bonds weren't there. Brandt picked up the empty satchel and stack of bonds and circled back to the car's passenger side.

Despite the innate analytical skills that helped to rapidly propel his career forward, Brandt tended to take a less nuanced approach to fighting crime. He kept it simple: crime is bad, criminals commit crime, criminals are bad. It was very black and white for him.

Brandt had done more than his fair share of self-reflection for a man in his late thirties. He'd reached the reasonable conclusion there was a disagreeable correlation between increased mental capability and practical application: the greater the ability to analyze, to discern, to understand, the greater the potential that shit didn't get done. He paid special attention when a peer announced a great idea to see if anything ever came of it; mostly not. He theorized, understandably, the genesis of his seemingly natural tendency to cut off the thinking and move forward with the action could be traced back to the ample time he spent as a child with his Cleveland iron worker father who was fully committed to his only son never spending one minute at dizzying heights over murky rivers for too little money, and dying too young from a broken-down body that inevitably quits quite unexpectedly. His son, the one who could think, would not be an iron worker.

Perhaps recognizing his son's inclination toward analysis, or maybe just because, Franklin Brandt frequently discouraged "overthinking," especially related to baseball, which they practiced endlessly in the empty lot next to the family home. The number of times Brandt's father urged him to "see the ball, catch the ball," and "see the ball, hit the ball," was inestimable. One simple directive Brandt liked as much as any was maybe the most logical: "If you watch the ball hit your bat, you'll never swing and miss." Damn, that sure made sense.

For Brandt it was all pretty simple. Jimmy is a criminal. Same for his wife or girlfriend or whatever, and same for the lowlife scum desperate for Hawkins' car. Brandt had a pretty good idea how things might go down in the West Bottoms that night. If Jimmy became a casualty, so be it.

"You finish up, Diehl. I'm taking your car to pick up the Chief and Cap."

"What?" Diehl was surprised. "Not a part of the plan, Brandt."

"Sorry, I failed to mention it," Brandt said, wiping his hands with a towel. "Chief's up to speed. He's waiting on me at HQ. Cap just got home from an evening out with his wife." Brandt read the skepticism on Diehl's face. "Look, Diehl, we're gonna need a couple extra sets of hands. Right?"

"Well, yeah, maybe so, but you've got a dozen suits right here."

"Yes, and no," Brandt said calmly. "First, most of 'em are gone for the evening and, second, this thing we got going on, the car, these particular bad guys, this is a need-to-know deal, and almost everyone here don't need to know."

Diehl just stared at Brandt for a moment, not happy at all being left in the dark, again, by someone he absolutely needed to trust, but recognizing whatever he thought, Cap and the department's Chief were going to be a part of the pinch. Plans evolve. He waved Brandt away. "Hustle back. We gotta get Jimmy over to the meet site a half-hour ahead."

"I'll be right back."

Paul looked at his watch. "Half past eleven, Vinny."

"What's the rush, Paul. We can be there in a jiff. Over to 12th, down the viaduct, south on Genessee a few blocks. Ten minutes tops."

Paul watched the big man roll up a fork full of pasta, poke a meatball, and stuff it all in his mouth. "Let's go, Vinny."

Still chewing, Vinny broke off a chunk of bread and crammed it in his mouth, drained his wine goblet and wiped his mouth. "Okay," he said, standing.

Brandt drove Diehl's car up to the garage door and tooted the horn. Inside, a young special agent slid the heavy door open, revealing Hawkins' Ford facing the street, Jimmy sitting in the passenger seat smoking a cigarette, looking cool as a cucumber.

Diehl and Brandt met at the door. Brandt nodded back at the Studebaker. "Cap and the Chief are up to speed."

"It's half past, Brandt. Better get going."

Diehl joined Chief Finney and Captain Mulroney, nodding to both. "Gentlemen." A strong odor of whiskey wafted from the back seat. "Doin' okay back there, Cap?"

Cap, arms crossed, squirmed a little before answering gruffly, "We'll talk first thing tomorrow."

Diehl backed out and drove the short distance on a deserted Genessee to the imposing Kansas City Livestock Exchange building, where he pulled up along the curb with a view east down 16th and, beyond, the hundreds of rail cars parked on thirty or so parallel spurs.

Just as Diehl killed the Studebaker's engine Brandt and Jimmy turned west onto 16th and motored forward half a block. Brandt killed the headlights, pulled the key from the ignition and got out of the car. After shutting the car door Brandt leaned in the window and checked on Jimmy. The yammering kid who wouldn't shut up an hour earlier, hadn't said a single word during the short drive from the garage. Brandt wasn't terribly worried about making the pinch. He was pretty certain that would go down as he expected, assuming the bad guys showed.

"Hey, kid," Brandt motioned, "slide over here. Sit in the driver's seat." He showed Jimmy the ignition key. "This'll be sitting on top of the rear tire. These guys wanna take the car, tell 'em where it's at. They wanna stiff you, let 'em stiff you. You try to run and I'll gun you down. Got it?"

"We're clear, copper," Jimmy said, tight-lipped, staring straight ahead.

"Okay, Jimmy, I'll be... "

Jimmy interrupted. "So they're givin' me three big ones for the car?"

Brandt whacked him across the forehead with the back of his hand. "Listen you dumb fuck, forget the goddamn money. Don't mess with these guys. Do what they say, walk away, and leave the rest to us."

Diehl watched through his binoculars as Brandt jogged east from Hawkins' car, crossing under a weak streetlight before disappearing into the shadows between two rail cars. Chief Finney, busy checking ammo in a revolver, looked over his shoulder through the rear window, then tapped Diehl on the shoulder and pointed behind them. Diehl leaned out the car window and looked back down Genessee. A pair of bouncing headlights, maybe three blocks away, approached at a decent speed.

"Think it's them, Diehl?" the Chief asked.

Diehl maneuvered to check his watch in the streetlamp's light. "Might be, but they're early." He watched as the car drew closer. "Chief, Cap, let's get low in our seats." The three men hunched down as Vinny and Paul slowed to turn east on 16th.

"There's the car, Vinny. Slow down." Paul squinted. "That car looks red, Vinny."

Vinny slowed as they approached Wyoming. "Oh yeah, the whore said they painted it red. That's gotta be it."

"Stop here at the corner, Vinny." Paul leaned forward, looking left and right down Wyoming. "Take a right, Vinny. Let's circle around behind it. Go slow."

Vinny turned south and drove slowly around the block while Paul carefully checked every doorway, every shadowy space for any sign of life, slowing to a stop at 16th where the two stared at the back of Hawkins' Ford. The inside of the red Ford illuminated briefly as Jimmy struck a match to light another Parliament, oblivious to the wary mobsters a hundred feet behind him. Smoke drifted from the car.

"The dame's a smoker?" Vinny asked.

"Hmm, no idea, Vinny," Paul answered, staring at the car. "Drive on down and circle back slow."

Hidden in the shadows under a rail car a stone's throw from the mobsters' car, Brandt watched intently as Vinny drove slowly north, then turned left and disappeared from sight. Less than a minute later Vinny turned slowly off Wyoming onto 16th and parked a few car lengths west of Jimmy, opposite side of the street, just as ordered by the demanding Glenda.

Vinny turned off the car's engine and headlights.

"Just one person, Paul."

"Yeah," Paul said as he studied the red Ford. "Stay here behind the wheel."

"You sure?"

"Stay here. I got this."

Paul pulled down the brim of his fedora and stepped out of the car, a small canvas bag in one hand. He straightened his jacket and moved confidently toward Hawkins' car. At the last moment he crossed in front of the car and stopped, staring intently at the shadowy figure behind the wheel.

Jimmy's hand trembled as he flicked his cigarette onto the street. Frozen by the gangster's set jaw, Jimmy shuddered as Paul placed the canvas bag on the car's hood and walked around to the passenger side door, leaning down to look inside. Jimmy stared straight ahead, terrified to make eye contact with the serious mobster.

"Where's the dame?" Paul demanded.

Jimmy struggled to answer, his voice breaking. "She sent me."

"Where is she?"

"I dunno," Jimmy finally answered.

Paul considered the answer. "Get outta the car," he ordered.

Jimmy fumbled with the door handle before tumbling out onto the street where he stood silently. Paul opened the passenger door and knelt down beside it. He ran his fingers along the lower edge of the door's panel. Paul found the cloth tab and gave it a tug, popping off the panel to reveal the secret compartment and the leather satchel, just as Gabe had described.

Jimmy glanced over his shoulder at the hulking dark figure behind the wheel of the mobsters' car, then watched in silence as Paul brought the satchel to the front of the car and flopped it down on the hood. The mobster unbuckled the straps and pulled out the stack of bonds, then turned to get some light on the bonds as he slowly fanned the stack. Satisfied he finally had the frustratingly elusive forged development bonds, Paul organized the stack and returned it to the satchel.

Half a block away, Brandt watched from the shadows as Jimmy stumbled out of the car and, a moment later, the gangster moved around to the front of the car. Still in a crouch next to a rail car, Brandt drew a .38 revolver and started inching forward. Almost two blocks due west, Diehl peered keenly at the scene through his binoculars, waiting for his cue to move.

Paul turned to Jimmy. "Get over here."

Jimmy hesitated. Paul lifted the canvas bag from the hood, moved out into the street and held it out. "Here's your money."

Jimmy walked forward slowly, finally reaching out for the bag. Just before Jimmy could grasp the bag, Paul dropped it. The bag plopped onto the dusty brick street.

"Oh shit," Brandt muttered to himself as he scrambled forward on the loose ballast.

Jimmy stared for a second at the bag on the street. The vise-like petrifying fear with which he'd been seized, disappeared in the blink of an eye. Disrespected by the smug city-boy, he was once again the small-town hot shot.

"Wrong move, city slicker," Jimmy said with a clenched jaw. He bent over and untied the canvas bag drawstring, pulling it open. Despite the limited light Jimmy could make out the Kansas City Star nameplate and a bold, front-page headline. He reached down into the bag. It was all newsprint.

Jimmy was seeing red. "You fuckin' . . . "

Paul's sucker punch was a blur, slamming like a hammer into Jimmy's chest below the sternum as he started to straighten up. For the tiniest fraction of a second half of Jimmy's brain urged him to leap up and start throwing haymakers, kick the pretty boy's ass, but the other half won out, the nervous system immediately shifting into a freeze and assess paralysis. Time slowed to slower than a crawl. Hunched over, mouth agape, Jimmy stared down at the mobster's spit-shined shoes, then to the mobster's fist glued to his chest.

Inside his chest Jimmy felt a sensation both cold and oddly ticklish, moving around, searching for something. Mesmerized, unable to move, Jimmy watched Paul's hand very slowly rotate one-quarter of a turn, then very slowly move to-and-fro as the six-inch, double-edge stiletto blade buried deep in Jimmy's chest searched for an obstruction, something that would block its path, his rubbery right ventricle. Finding it, Paul violently shoved the blade upward, then ripped it downward and out of Jimmy's chest, slicing open the organ like a hot knife through butter.

Jimmy felt an immediate, soothing rush of warmth spread throughout his chest. He stared down at the blood-covered stiletto, thick red drops falling slowly from the blade to the street, as intensely bright, microscopic-size flashes erupted at the edges of his vision, growing exponentially in number toward the center, quickly shrouding his eyes. Darkness followed.

"What's wrong rube, cat got your tongue," Paul sneered as he stepped back, watching Jimmy drop to his knees and fall face-first onto the street. Paul dropped the stiletto next to the twitching body and reached into a pocket for a clean handkerchief, but was startled by Vinny yelling and scrambling to open the car door, another car roaring toward them from the west, footsteps and yelling from behind him.

Diehl dropped the binoculars and fired up the Studebaker's engine when he saw Brandt sprinting out of the rail yard. The car's tires squealed as he jerked the wheel and floored it down 16th, still picking up speed as he flew through the Wyoming intersection and slammed on the brakes, skidding sideways to a halt behind the mobsters' car, the Studebaker's headlights illuminating the grisly scene. Diehl and the Chief threw open their doors and leaped from the car, guns drawn on Vinny. Seconds before, Paul turned toward the commotion behind him to find Brandt almost on top of him, a badge in one hand and a revolver trained on his chest in the other. Without a struggle, the mobsters raised their hands overhead.

Though winded from flying down the street, Brandt screamed, "On the ground! Now!" Slowly, the two dropped to their knees, then laid down flat.

Diehl trained his gun on Vinny. "Cap, get over here and cuff him, search him. Chief, keep a gun on him." Relieved by the Chief, Diehl holstered his weapon and stepped over to Jimmy. He knelt down and rolled over the blood-soaked, limp body. The kid's lifeless eyes stared skyward. Instinctively, he felt for the pulse he knew he wouldn't find.

Rising, Diehl stepped over Jimmy's body to Paul, now cuffed and on his feet, standing next to Brandt. Before Brandt could react, Diehl grabbed the young mobster's collar, jerked him away from Brandt's reach, and with all of his body weight slammed the cold-blooded killer face first into the red Ford. Paul bounced off the car's body, slumping to the ground.

"Diehl, no!" Brandt yelled, rushing forward. He helped the dazed and bloodied mobster to his feet. "Damn it, Diehl. Fuck." Brandt pulled out his handkerchief and gingerly daubed a flow of blood from Paul's nose. "Search him, Diehl." Brandt ordered, stepping back.

Diehl did a thorough search from ankles to the nape of the neck, finding only a money clip and thick wad of bills. "He's clean."

"Bring him over here, Diehl," Brandt ordered, pointing to a spot in the middle of the street. "Cap, bring me the muscle."

Cap and the Chief led Vinny toward Brandt. "That's good right there, Cap," Brandt said, stepping up to Paul's smug partner. "I'm guessing it was you who popped Gabe Hawkins," Brandt said to him.

Vinny didn't react, staring past Brandt.

"A shot to the head, one to the heart, stuffed him in an old oil drum, rolled him into the river behind the family salvage yard? That how it went down, Vincenzo?"

Vinny reacted to his name, locking eyes with Brandt.

"Yeah, Vinny boy, the barrel never sank. Oops. Made it a couple hundred yards downstream and got hung up along the bank," Brandt said calmly. "A river rat checking his trotlines found it this morning."

Brandt grabbed Vinny by his tie and led him next to Paul. "Keep an eye on 'em, Diehl," Brandt said, turning to Cap and Chief Finney. "Any weapons?" Brandt asked, holding out a hand. The Chief handed over Vinny's .22 revolver, a set of brass knuckles, a pearl-handled switch blade, and a two-shot derringer they found in a holster strapped to the big man's ankle.

Brandt pocketed the brass knuckles, knife and derringer, checked the revolver's rounds, flipped the revolver's cylinder closed, cocked the gun's hammer, stepped back and, in one fluid motion, raised the gun and fired a single shot into the middle of Cap's forehead, the loud "crack" piercing the West Bottoms late-night stillness.

"No!" a stunned Diehl screamed, not believing what he'd just seen. He jumped toward Brandt, but Chief Finney cut him off, locking the young detective in a tight bear-hug.

"Jesus Christ, what're you doing?" Diehl yelled at Brandt, squirming to free himself from the Chief's hold.

Brandt ignored Diehl as he knelt down and removed Cap's revolver, laying it on the street next to his body. Brandt straightened up, turned and walked past Chief Finney and the writhing Diehl toward the stunned gangsters, unholstering the .38 revolver as he stopped three paces short, leveled the gun and "bang, bang, bang," fired three shots into Vinny's chest, the force of the slugs driving the made man back a step before he toppled over flat onto his back.

Brandt stared at the horrified Paul as he walked past him, briefly standing over Vinny's dying body. Blood gurgled from the big man's mouth, his body twitched once, twice, then went limp.

Brandt turned back toward Paul. Still holding the revolver, Brandt leaned forward. "Eureka," Brandt said. He waited for a response, some sense of recognition. He said it again, but a little louder this time. "Eureka." Brandt stared intently, patiently waiting. Then it happened. Paul's tense facial features relaxed and a slight smile creased his face. "Stay here, Paulie boy," Brandt ordered. "We got a train to catch."

Diehl sensed the Chief's bear-hug loosen as Brandt turned from the surviving mobster and started toward them. Figuring he was next, Diehl made a sudden move, wresting himself free and, stumbling forward on the street, unholstered his weapon, straightening up to find Brandt standing mere feet away, his revolver pointed at Diehl's head.

Chief Finney leapt between the two. "No!" he screamed. "Diehl, stand down."

The Chief slowly extended an open hand to Diehl. "Give me your gun, son."

Brandt lowered his weapon a little. "Diehl," he said, calmly. "I've never seen anyone dirty as Cap. Not even close. I did the piece of shit a favor. He should be headed to Lansing. Now the piece of shit gets the bagpipes and a statue. His widow gets his pension."

The three men stood frozen in place for another second or two before Brandt turned his back on the others and walked over to Hawkins' car, snatched the satchel from the hood, then stepped to the rear tire for the ignition key. He fished his cuff key from a pants pocket, walked over to Paul and uncuffed him.

The distant wail of a squad car siren from atop Quality Hill on the West Bottoms' Missouri side stopped everyone in their tracks. The sound echoed down the narrow valley as the squad car raced down the 12th Street viaduct, only a few blocks north.

"We gotta move, Paulie boy," Brandt said. "Get in the car. Move!"

Brandt stepped over to Chief Finney, ignoring Diehl. "Here's your gun, Chief," he said, handing the .38 to him, taking in exchange the .38 revolver Chief Finney removed from his holster.

"Chief, get the cuffs off Vinny," Brandt directed, then pointed to the stiletto laying near Jimmy's body. "The poker's got Jimmy's blood on it. Vinny's right hand doesn't. The .22, too. The car'll be at Union Station." Then he turned to Diehl. "Chief does the talkin', all of it. Chief writes the report. Nothin' good happens if you do the Boy Scout thing, Diehl."

Diehl wanted to smash Brandt's face, wanted to kill the heartless son-of-a-bitch, but did nothing. He'd never felt such anger, but didn't flinch a muscle. He just stared as Brandt jumped in the red Ford and raced away.

Brandt rattled off instructions as he sped through the city's late-night traffic. "Train's not rolling 'til we board," he said, handing Paul a sleeping compartment ticket. "You're gonna call your old man before we board. He'll arrange a ride for you there in Chicago." Brandt pulled some coins from his coat packet and handed them to Paul.

"Got it?"

Paul nodded.

"Your old man's expecting your call. We clear?"

Again, Paul nodded.

# WEST BOTTOMS

# THURSDAY, JULY 12, 1934, MIDDAY

At noon, following an uneventful trip, Brandt blended in with a knot of other recent arrivals and followed several paces back as Paul stepped out of Dearborn Station into downtown Chicago's mix of bright sunlight and welcome shade. Along the street curb, Angelo Ricitti, leaning against his car's fender, removed his hat and waved until Paul saw him, then opened the passenger side door and hustled around to the driver's side.

"Welcome back, Paulie," Ricitti said with a broad smile as he eased the car into traffic. "A friend in Cowtown tells me you've been busy."

Paul ignored the clumsy attempt to pry information. "What's happened on this end, Fist? Where's 'Two Chins'?"

"Your father asked me to leave Tommy at home. Just you 'n' me. What's been happenin' here? Hmm, well, Tommy and me went to do some investing business with our broker friend. Couple days ago. No appointment. Slipped in, slipped out." Ricitti laughed. "Yeah, he figured we were bringin' more paper." Ricitti laughed again as he recalled the broker's horror when he realized the meeting's purpose.

"And?" Paul asked.

"Well, Tommy knocked him cold with one punch, we opened a window and tossed him out. Eight floors down to the sidewalk. Splat! Headfirst. Sounded like a smashed melon." Ricitti paused. "Get this, Paulie, he landed at the feet of a flatfoot. Almost took out a copper!"

Paul sat in silence, imagining the broker going about his business one moment, then hurtling to his death the next. The rube, swapping a car for cash one moment, then gushing blood onto a Kansas City street the next. Lives that existed for years, meant something to someone, gone without warning, without a say in it.

Ricitti continued. "Papers say it's suicide. Coppers are investigating, but no evidence of a struggle and no leads."

"Good," Paul said, withdrawing again to silence.

The balance of the drive to meet with Paul's father was filled with periods of silence, broken by Ricitti's rambling monologue about the Cubs' unlikely pennant prospects and his disturbing fling with a precocious teenage cousin.

"Here we go, Paulie," Ricitti said as he parked under a shady elm outside the Bunicci home. "Know why we're meeting, Paulie?"

"Not specifically," Paul answered as he tightened his silk tie knot and picked up the satchel. "Let's go."

Paul's mother stepped out onto the porch with a loving smile, arms outstretched. "My boys," she said, hugging each warmly. "Come in, come in."

Inside the home, Tony Bunicci, dressed casually and smiling broadly, stood at the door to his study. "Join me, please." After hugging each of the younger men Tony followed them into his study, closing and locking the door behind him.

Tony motioned to the two chairs facing his desk. "Sit, sit, please."

Tony checked his watch as he moved around the desk and sat down. "So, son, our friend in Kansas City speaks very highly of you. Last night was unfortunate, though."

"Yes, and there's a couple loose ends back there we need to address," Paul reported. "Our Canadian friend? Is he a loose end?"

Tony smiled. "There are always loose ends, right Angelo?"

Angelo chuckled. "Yessir."

"Our Canadian friend?" Tony reflected, "No, no, he is not a loose end. He is closed down for now, but we may need him again. He is very gifted, and he will not talk."

As was his custom, Tony turned to Paul and cut to the chase. "Did you find our missing package?"

"I have it here, pops," Paul answered, laying the satchel on the desk, sliding it toward his father.

The old man leaned forward, unbuckled the satchel straps and removed the stack of counterfeit bonds. He pulled a bond from the top of the stack and laid it off to the side, swiveled around in his chair, fanned out the stack and tossed it all into the fireplace. Swiveling back to his desk, Tony opened a drawer and removed a small tin of kerosene and box of matches. He swiveled back to the fireplace and liberally sprinkled the toxic-smelling kerosene across the papers, emptying the tin.

Swiveling back to his desk Tony set the tin aside, vigorously wiped his hands with a cloth, then rolled up the remnant counterfeit bond. Striking a match, Tony lit the end of the rolled bond, rotating it slowly until the flame took hold. He swiveled slowly back to the fireplace and, leaning back, tossed the burning bond onto the kerosene-soaked papers.

"Whoosh!" A sudden burst of flame completely filled the firebox, shooting out into the study a spike of intense heat that died back almost as quickly as it appeared. Tony leaned over and grabbed the fireplace poker, stirring the swiftly burning paper, careful all was being consumed. Finally satisfied, Tony turned back to Paul and Angelo. "A lesson we best learn early," Tony said, "is hogs get slaughtered, pigs live another day."

Ricitti looked confused, Paul smiled.

Tony continued. "This caper played out well for us. Might we have done better, made more money? Of course. But it ran its course. There was always an end date. We just didn't know when that time would come." He paused, looking at Paul. "So, we live another day."

Before Tony could share with his youngest son more of the knowledge gained over a lifetime, the moment was abruptly interrupted by banging on the home's front door. Paul and Ricitti tensed up.

"Police, open up!" a man's voice boomed from the porch.

Tony calmly motioned the two to stay seated as he rose from his chair and walked to the study door. He unlocked and opened the door, stepping into the hallway. "It's okay, dear," he said to his wife waiting near the front door.

"Let him in. Bring him to us."

Tony returned to his chair as the ominous sound of a single set of heavy footsteps stopped at the study doorway. Paul and Ricitti turned in their seats as Brandt filled the doorway, his Division of Intelligence badge in one hand, in the other a .38 revolver. "Brandt, Special Agent," he announced, noting the stench of kerosene and the smoldering pile of ash in the fireplace. "A little warm for a fire, don't you think?"

The mobsters didn't respond. After an awkward moment, Tony broke the silence. "How can we help, Special Agent Brandt?"

Brandt pocketed his badge and raised the revolver to his waist. "Hands on the desk. Now!" The mobsters obeyed.

Brandt moved into the study, closing the door behind him. Cautiously, he stepped forward and lifted Hawkins' empty satchel from the desk. "It's empty," Brandt muttered to himself. "This have anything to do with that smokin' ash?"

No one answered.

"You packin', Fist?" Brandt asked gruffly.

Ricitti stared straight ahead, ignoring the question, then shrugged dismissively when Paul urged under his breath, "Tell him, Fist."

The disrespect wasn't lost on Brandt. In two quick steps he moved behind the huge capo and, in a fluid motion, pivoted and with all the force he could muster, swung the butt of his .38 into the side of the big man's head, knocking him from his chair.

The sudden violence startled Paul, sending him back in his chair, almost tumbling over. Brandt trained his gun on Tony, then Paul, then Tony, then returned his attention to Ricitti. "Get up, Fist," he ordered, grabbing him by the back of his shirt collar, helping the dazed mobster to his feet. "Hands behind your head!"

Brandt pushed the muzzle of his revolver into the back of Ricitti's neck, reaching around him to feel for his piece. Brandt pulled a .22 revolver from a holster on Ricitti's waist, flipped the cylinder open, quickly checked the rounds, then flipped the cylinder closed.

Brandt took a step back. "Turn around, Fist," Brandt ordered, taking another step back.

Hands still behind his head, Angelo turned slowly around to face Brandt. Brandt fired a round from Ricitti's revolver into the study floor. The mobsters jumped at the unexpected, deafening "pop." Then, quick as lightning Brandt raised his .38 and fired three quick, window-rattling rounds into the middle of the big man's chest. "Boom! Boom! Boom!"

Outside the study Mrs. Bunicci shrieked, then let out a blood-curdling scream. Paul toppled over awkwardly as he scrambled away from the gunfire, and Tony winced with each round. Ricitti staggered backward as the slugs slammed into his chest, then fell in a heap near the fireplace.

Brandt stepped over to Ricitti, knelt down beside the dying capo and laid the .22 revolver on the floor near his right hand. Brandt pointed to Ricitti's right hand and looked up at Tony, who nodded.

"My God," Paul muttered, now back on his feet, looking at his father, then Brandt. "Another lesson, pops?"

Tony ignored his favorite son's cynicism, moving a foot to avoid the slowly expanding pool of blood.

Before more could be said the men were interrupted by loud crashing from outside the room as the front door was kicked in, followed by shouting voices, rushing footsteps, and a study full of agents, guns drawn. Brandt stepped back into a corner of the study as the half-dozen special agents filled the room, quickly searching and cuffing Tony and Paul. "What about the woman?" one asked Brandt, nodding toward the open door where a horrified Mrs. Bunicci stood wide-eyed.

Brandt looked at her. "No, not her."

"This one's dead," another special agent said, kneeling at Ricitti's body.

"Dave," Brandt said as Tony and Paul were being led out into the hallway, "put the young one in the back seat of my car."

"You got it, boss."

As the study emptied out, Brandt stood quietly, contemplating the carnage he'd wrought, pulled his notepad from a breast pocket and scribbled a few notes. On the front porch, manned by two serious-looking special agents, Brandt stopped to survey a scene both dynamic and static. Car doors slamming shut, wailing distant sirens, a tan coupe screeching to a stop, a local reporter and young photographer piling out of it, cars roaring away down an otherwise quiet street one might find anywhere in middle-class America.

In contrast, up and down the street, the Bunicci neighbors had gathered, silently gawking at the spectacle certain to splash across the evening paper's front page.

Brandt lit a cigarette, stepped off the front porch and walked uninterrupted across the street to his parked car. He opened the driver's side door and leaned inside. "It's okay, Dave," he said to the young special agent sitting in the front passenger seat, "I got him. Catch another ride."

"You sure?"

Brandt didn't answer.

"Okay, boss, see you downtown."

Brandt slid into the driver's seat, closed the door, took a final draw from his cigarette and flicked it out onto the street. After exhaling out the car window he turned to face his prisoner.

"Here's how it's going to go, kid. You and your daddy are gonna be booked, printed, photographed, maybe interviewed. Depends on how fast your high-priced mouthpiece can get down to the courthouse." Brandt paused. "You followin' me so far?"

Paul, expressionless, stared straight ahead.

"Good, good," Brandt continued. "They say you're smart like your old man. Just keep doin' that Omerta thing and you'll both be out on the sidewalk before supper, and there'll never be a trial."

Paul twitched but remained silent.

"Kid, your daddy's taking your momma to the Keys, or someplace down in Florida where it doesn't snow, and they ain't comin' back. I guess you know that." Brandt studied the young mobster for a sign. Nothing. "Or maybe you don't. Least not yet."

Brandt started the car engine, adjusted the rearview mirror, and eased forward. "So, no more wars, no more massacres, no more fuckin' headlines." Brandt checked Paul in the mirror. "You got it?"

Paul stared straight ahead.

"Here's the deal, kid, you fuck with me and I'll come down on you like a sack of rocks. But, you stay outta the headlines and, well, we'll both do what we gotta do."

Brandt slowed for a stop sign and pulled several folded pages of heavy parchment from his breast pocket. Unfolding the papers, he held up one of the counterfeit bonds for Paul to see.

"Here's the deal, kid, Mr. Hoover owns you now."

## NANA'S STORY, PART FIVE

"**N**ana, so no one else who knows what you're telling me?"

"Prob'ly not, Sweetie. Again, we're talkin' 70 years ago." Foxy thought for a moment. "Jimmy was dead before I reached California, and after I got out here the only person I told anything to was Big Jimmy."

"What'd you tell him, Nana?"

"Well, we'd been married a couple years, and I couldn't shake the guilt, hiding my past from him. So I told him. Told him everything. Plus, I never knew how Jimmy died 'cause a newspaper article I tracked down was totally wrong. Made up. A lie." Foxy stopped for a sip of her drink. "So, I told Big Jimmy about the G-men and Jimmy dying, and asked if he could find out what really happened." Foxy smiled. "Typical Big Jimmy, he just said 'sure,' he'd make a few calls."

"What did he find out?"

"I dunno. A few days later, maybe a week, we're eating supper at home and Big Jimmy says 'you know that Kansas City thing?' I said 'yeah.' And between bites he says, 'for your safety, Little Jimmy's safety, my safety, we never speak of it again, to anyone,' and then he keeps on eating."

"Oh my, Nana, so you still don't know?"

"No, Cupcake, that's for you to find out."

"Okay, so what about the G-men, Nana?" Megan looked up from her notepad. "And, uh, what exactly are G-men?"

"The FBI. Federal cops. So, we've got Jimmy's market, everything's hunky-dory, and two nights later I'm in a spooky warehouse filled with G-men, in a room by myself, one hand cuffed to a cheap chair, chain-smoking Camels.

I've spilled my guts. Told 'em everything. Next stop is up the river to women's prison."

"Warehouse? The FBI has you in a warehouse? That doesn't make sense. You sure these were the FBI?"

Foxy laughed. "Mr. Hoover's dress code. Hoover was their big boss. Anyway, all of 'em looked the same. White dress shirt, tie, young, clean-cut." Foxy paused. "Save for the older one, Munchkin. I got a look at him when they brought us in, me and Jimmy, but didn't see him again until late that night." Foxy stopped again, took a drag, then recalled the moment. "It was past midnight. I'd nodded off. The door opens behind me, waking me up. It was the older one. He unlocked the handcuff, freeing my hand, and left, leaving the door to the room wide open. I just sit there, looking at the doorway. A moment later he was back in the doorway. We stared at each other. He spoke this time, no nonsense, very serious. 'Jimmy's dead, the back door's unlocked, leave Kansas City and never come back. Now.'" Foxy smiled wryly. "So I did."

Megan checked her watch. "Mother and Father should be arriving pretty soon, Nana."

"And you've got your story. Promise me you'll write it."

"I will, Nana. I promise."

"And, Megan, find out what happened to my Jimmy Dale."

## SUNDAY, JULY 22, 1934, EVENING

Diehl knelt next to the narrow stream. An early evening, gentle breeze rustled leaves of the trees that shielded him and Lulu from the setting Kansas sun. Diehl stealthily lifted a small flat rock at the stream's edge with his left hand, the thumb and fingers of his right hand poised just above the water, ready to pounce.

"Got it," Diehl exclaimed gleefully, shooting upright with the squirming crawdad he'd plucked from the water. He swung around to his sister, holding out the slimy crustacean.

"Eeeek," Lulu squealed, leaning back on the felled log where she sat. "Get that nasty thing away from me."

Diehl smiled, turning to gently return the traumatized crawdad to its watery home. He set it at the water's edge and watched as it scurried to the safety of water-logged leaves. Wiping his wet hand on his shorts, Diehl stood and stepped back from the stream, joining his little sister on the log.

"Were you scared?" he asked.

"Oh my God, of course," Lulu answered. I thought you'd bite my head off when I called to tell you she was gone."

"No, dumbass, not that. Talkin' to the gangsters. Were you scared?"

"Of course I was scared, but not about being Glenda. I nailed that drawl down quick. That southern accent, her attitude, only took me a few minutes. Once I started being her, my confidence shot way up. My goodness, it was empowering. That's weird, right?"

"No, I think I get it."

Lulu thought about the momentous evening. She arrived to an empty house.

Glenda, Bobby Joe, Mary Jo, had fled. Turns out Glenda was needed to set up the stolen car transfer. No call from Glenda and the bad guys escape justice. Satisfied she could pass for Glenda, Lulu took a deep breath and dialed the telephone number for Tallman's Grill. A raspy voice answered. "Yeah, whadda ya want?"

"I wanna speak to Vinny," Lulu answered firmly with her best Glenda drawl. Then she upped it a few notches with the backwoods swagger she imagined was the real Glenda. "Tell him it's Glenda. I can get him the car he's lookin' for. Now!"

"Uh, hold on."

A moment later another voice spoke to her. "Hullo."

"Who's this?" Lulu demanded.

"This is Vinny."

"I gotta message for Paul. Got a pencil, Vinny. Can you write?"

"What the –"

"Shuddup, Vinny. Here's how it's gonna go. Want the car? Here's what you gotta do."

Lulu laughed, elbowing her big brother. "Yup, I was scared until I got going." She paused. "You know, it's just like going on stage. I get a lot of butterflies, but once I start, I'm fine."

"You were great last night, by the way."

"Ahh, thank you, donkey poop." Lulu remembered something. "Oh, oh, guess what?" she asked excitedly.

"What?"

"Jacob, Mr. Greenberg, loved my bit. He's giving me more minutes next weekend. He loved the Eleanor Roosevelt shtick about the poodle and the cat."

"Now that was funny. The whole place erupted."

"I had one more bit, but after I heard the crowd laughing so hard I figured it was a good place to end it." Lulu added. "Here's what I've been thinking. Instead of it being me that walks out on stage, I'll be Glenda that walks out on stage. I really need to use her, but she's not famous."

Diehl thought about it for moment. "I like it, kiddo. Excellent idea."

"Think we'll ever see her again?" Lulu asked.

"If she's smart, she's on her way to a cabin in Montana." Diehl shuddered at what might happen if Glenda ever grew complacent, stopped looking behind her back.

"So, the small-town guy's dead. I read about it in the paper. Article said he had a moll. Is she going to prison?"

Diehl forced himself to revisit the unbelievably insane late night in the West Bottoms. Three cold-blooded murders, including Cap. The Missouri side's finest crawling all over the gruesome scene, shepherding away the drunk onlookers, doing their best to shoo away the snoopy press, the incessant popping sound of flashbulbs. He'd wanted to walk away but, instead, he dutifully stood by Chief Finney's side as the Chief spun a rehearsed yarn about a sting to bring down a loan-sharking ring, a stolen car to pay a debt, and the heroic Cap giving his life to nab the bad guys.

Just as Brandt predicted, Cap got a jam-packed funeral with all the honors: bagpipes, rifle salute, taps, and a huge turnout of the area's grateful public. A future statue to the man would not be a surprise.

As for Nancy Gleason, the Chief and Diehl returned to the DOI's nondescript command center first thing the next morning and she was gone, like a ghost. No one there seemed to know anything about her, or so they said. There was no sign of the written, signed confessions, and no one seemed to know anything about those, either.

"The dead kid's moll?" Diehl answered. "Well, who knows?"

"Hold on, you won't tell me anything?"

"We did recover the stolen car, though it's not clear just yet who'll end up with it. Beyond that, I can't tell ya. I promise, you don't wanna know."

"Wow, that's a mood killer," Lulu said, laughing. "So, what's next for you?"

"Well, the Chief says he's not gonna accept my resignation. He mailed this to me a couple days ago," Diehl said, pulling a folded envelope from his pocket.

"What is it?"

"He wants me to take Cap's place. Says he wants me to do things different, and he'll give me total say on doing it. Change how we hire, how we promote. He thinks we're hiring head-busters and then expecting 'em to grow into detectives, instead of hiring future detectives capable of busting heads. Makes sense."

"So, you're going to do it, not do it?"

"I'm not sure. I'm still thinkin' about it. I called, we talked, told him I need a few more days." Diehl said, but failed to add a mere two hours after speaking by telephone with the Chief he'd received a cryptic cable from Special Agent Brandt, hand-delivered to his home in a plain envelope by a well-dressed young man who knocked on Diehl's door, handed over the envelope, politely tipped the brim of his hat, turned around and left without saying a word. The message was like a clue from a Dashiell Hammett detective novel: "Topeka, July 16, shoe salesman shot dead."

Curious about Brandt's mysterious note, Diehl tracked down a newspaper story describing the brazen, broad daylight shooting of a young shoe salesman walking home from his job at Macy's in downtown Topeka. He hailed from an influential Kansas City family. Topeka police are baffled.

"Kids," their mother called out from up near the house.

"Yes, Mother," Lulu shouted back.

"Supper's ready, and your father's hungry. We'll be eating on the patio."

"We'll be right up," Diehl shouted.

"What did you get Father for his birthday?" Lulu asked.

"He's been grumbling about his rain gauge. Says it's not accurate. So I got him a fancy, pricey one. He'll like it. How 'bout you?"

"You remember when we were kids and he would always be telling us when it was the winter solstice, or the autumnal equinox, or whatever?" They both laughed. "Heck," Lulu continued, "I couldn't even spell 'solstice' until I was in high school. So, I got him a sundial that sits on a pedestal. Also fancy, also pricey. I think he'll love it."

"Yeah, he'll love it. Let's go eat."

## THE END

WEST BOTTOMS

# ABOUT THE AUTHORS

*Rogers Brazier* is a lifelong Kansan, raised in McPherson and Wamego, with degrees in political science (Kansas State University) and the law (Washburn University of Topeka). After thirty years in Topeka and a varied career working with awesome people, he's now happily retired, living for more than a decade in the wonderful small town of Burlingame. His passions include sports, reading, learning, following the markets, serving his formerly homeless cats, and staying active. Rogers has two adult daughters of whom he's incredibly proud: Morgan (and Josh) in Illinois, and Hayley (and Thomas) in Oregon. He has a grandson, Theo, and a granddaughter, Spencer.

*Mace Thornton* is a former journalist, an author, and strategic communications specialist. His debut novel, ***Jawbone Holler***, was published in 2024. A native of Troy, Kansas, he grew up on a small farm in the Missouri River Hills of northeast Kansas. With a degree in journalism from Benedictine College in Atchison, Kan., among his passions are writing, sports, and the people of agriculture. His award-winning journalism and commentaries have been published across the nation. His career took him far away from his home state for more than three decades, but he now lives a little closer, in the St. Louis area with his wife, Denise, and their spirited

rescue pup, Anna Mae. In addition to writing, he is a partner at Stratovation Group, a research, marketing, and communications firm headquartered in Columbus, Ohio. The Thorntons have three adult children scattered to the corners of our great nation: Trace (and Amy) in Virginia, Troy (and Katrina) in Washington state, and Taylor (and Shawn) in Georgia. They also have one granddaughter, Grace.

# WEST BOTTOMS

www.ingramcontent.com/pod-product-compliance
Lightning Source LLC
Chambersburg PA
CBHW031953010726
47493CB00007B/2186